"Can't sleep?"

Her heart picked up its pace as Jake stood and crossed the small kitchen to stand in front of her. The single bulb that had seemed bright before now shone like a spotlight, emphasizing his tousled dark blond hair, the rough stubble emphasising his jaw, the naked chest only inches away, and Sophia couldn't look away.

"Sophia." His voice held a hint of warning, and her gaze instantly rose to meet his. The desire she saw there only amplified the longing spinning through her in ever tightening circles, spiralling down into a pinpoint focus. She wanted him to kiss her. To let the heat and urgency of his mouth against hers wipe away the past weeks. To turn back time to those few, short days when Jake Cameron was a man she could trust, a man she could count on…

Instead of a man who lied.

Dear Reader,

Are you the oldest? The middle? How about the youngest? Research says birth order can affect personality. Firstborns can be demanding, always wanting their way. Second children can be easygoing and seek to avoid confrontation. (Okay, I admit, that's me!) Then, you have the last born. The baby left to follow in her siblings' footsteps or break out on her own.

Sophia Pirelli is the last born *and* the only girl. Her attempt to break away and find her own place hasn't worked out. Now, she's returned home to celebrate her parents' anniversary...and tell her family about her unplanned pregnancy.

When Jake Cameron meets pregnant Sophia, he's certain he isn't the man for her. Experience has taught him he's not a forever guy. But he'll step in as her fiancé until he can convince Sophia her hometown is the perfect place for her and her baby. Only the more time they spend together, the more Sophia sees Jake in a permanent role—as her husband!

I hope you enjoy Sophia and Jake's journey to finding their own place in the family they create together.

Stacy Connelly

Her Fill-In Fiancé

STACY CONNELLY

First published in Great Britain 2011
by Mills & Boon, an imprint of Harlequin (UK) Limited,
Large Print edition 2011
Eton House, 18-24 Paradise Road,
Richmond, Surrey TW9 1SR

© Stacy Cornell 2011

ISBN: 978 0 263 22273 9

Harlequin (UK) policy is to use papers that are natural,
renewable and recyclable products and made from
wood grown in sustainable forests. The logging
and manufacturing process conform to the legal
environmental regulations of the country of origin.

Printed and bound in Great Britain
by CPI Antony Rowe, Chippenham, Wiltshire

STACY CONNELLY

has dreamed of publishing books since she was a kid, writing stories about a girl and her horse. Eventually, boys made it onto the page as she discovered a love of romance and the promise of happily ever after.

When she is not lost in the land of make-believe, Stacy lives in Arizona with her two spoiled dogs. She loves to hear from readers and can be contacted at stacyconnelly@cox.net or www.stacyconnelly.com

To Christine—

Thanks for sharing
your hometown with me.

Chapter One

Pulling into a circa-1950 gas station thirty miles from her hometown, Sophia Pirelli drove to the first of two pumps and dropped her head back against the seat. Tall pines lined the roadside and dotted distant hills. A slight breeze carried their scent, as well as a hint of salt and sand and sea. So close to home, yet she was tempted to gas up and floor it back to St. Louis, where she'd been staying with her cousin, or…or anywhere other than here.

As much as she loved her family, another trip home filled with worried looks and sympathetic, sorrowful "Oh, Sophias" from her parents might be more than she could take. Add in the "I told you so" times three from her older brothers, and she didn't know how she'd make it through the visit. She could hear Sam, Drew and Nick already.

I told you you wouldn't like Chicago.

I knew you'd hate being a live-in maid, surrounded by strangers.

If only you'd listened when we told you to stay home.

If only she'd listened…

Her life's list of *if onlys* ran the length of her arm, down to the ring she wore as a constant reminder of regret and past mistakes. Sophia twirled the silver band with her thumb as she climbed from the car. She'd known she couldn't stay away forever, but the nerves tearing her up inside reminded her the old saying was true.

"You can't go home again," she murmured as she swiped her credit card.

And as if this first visit home in two years wasn't going to be hard enough, she had an unplanned pregnancy to confess. Despite the three over-the-counter tests, the doctor's confirmation and her undeniable morning sickness, Sophia still had a hard time believing she was pregnant. She was alternately thrilled and terrified with both emotions sometimes overwhelming her at once.

But if the idea that she would soon be a mother felt like something out of a dream, then the two months since discovering her pregnancy were straight from a nightmare. She could only imagine the explanation she'd have to give her family.

Yeah, you guys were right. Chicago never did feel like home. I hated living in the Dunworthy mansion surrounded by people who treated me like I was miles beneath them. So, I guess it's just as well that I got fired for "seducing" Todd, the family's youngest son, who just so happens to be the father of the child I'm carrying.

That was all a bit much, even for her. Still, she would have to tell them, but not until after her parents' anniversary party. Their thirty-fifth anniversary…

Vince and Vanessa Pirelli had a great deal to show for those thirty-five years—a strong, love-filled marriage, three handsome, successful sons who lived and worked in their hometown. Nick, the oldest, was the town's vet. Drew owned his own construction company. Sam was a top mechanic. And then there was Sophia, the baby and black sheep of the family.

She refused to cast a pall over this celebration. She'd done enough of that as a teenager.

"Well, well, if it isn't little Sophia Pirelli."

The mocking comment carried across ten feet of asphalt from the small glass-front shop stocked with beer, cigarettes and travel-sized necessities. Sophia didn't recognize the voice, but it hardly mattered. She turned to face the uniformed attendant, who obviously recognized her. She sneaked a glance at the ragged name tag tacked to the gray, button-down shirt as the man swaggered toward her and wracked her brain for a memory of the brawny, dirty blond-haired man named Bob.

Drawing a blank, she forced a smile and said,

"That's right. You were in my brother's class at Clearville High, weren't you?"

Her three older brothers' combined high school careers spanned nine years. It was a good guess that this man had been a classmate to one if not two of them, but not enough to cover her lack of recognition.

The man gave a scoffing laugh. "You always did think you were too good for the rest of us," he almost spat.

Heat climbed to Sophia's cheeks. Any number of denials rose to her throat, but they would have all been lies. Truth was, she *had* thought she was too good for her small hometown, certain bigger and better things existed in the world outside its close-knit confines, and in high school, she'd made little secret of how she'd felt.

"You and Amy Leary were the Clearville queens, treating the rest of us like your pawns. You didn't care who got hurt."

And that was the worst of it, Sophia thought, memories crowding around her until she felt trapped, suffocated. *People* had *gotten hurt.*

"Look, Bob—"

"My name is Jeff," he ground out.

She closed her eyes briefly. "Of course it is," she murmured beneath her breath, knowing nothing she said would change this man's opinion of her. An opinion too many people in town shared.

"But you're not so high and mighty now, are you? I heard you're nothing but a maid, scrubbing rich people's gold-trimmed toilets."

The implied insult stung. Being a maid had never been her dream job, but it was a job that, until Todd came along, she'd done quietly, anonymously, blending into the background, unnoticed by those around her. Almost as if the uniform had the power to make her invisible, which had been fine with Sophia.

After everything that happened in the months before she left Clearville, she'd wanted little more than to disappear.

Reminding herself she'd faced far harsher criticism than anything Bob/Jeff could dole out, she lifted her chin and said, "Actually, I'm not a maid anymore." A hollow victory since she was unemployed instead, but he didn't need to know that.

Looking disappointed that his *gold-trimmed toilets* comment had gone to waste, Jeff demanded, "So what are you doing?"

"Buying gas," she said as she reached past him and grabbed the pump, "so I can go home to visit my family."

Maybe it was the reminder of her family, of her brothers, but the man gave her a last disgruntled look before lumbering around to the back of the small shop. For Sophia, though, the damage was already done. Her hand shook so badly it took three tries to get the pump into the tank, and the knots tightening her stomach made morning sickness seem no worse than a hiccup.

Knowing she needed a break before climbing back behind the wheel for the final leg of her journey, Sophia hesitantly approached the shop. She half expected Jeff to jump out from the side of the building and bar her way, but she slipped inside unnoticed. The young girl behind the register didn't look up from her phone, her fingers flying across the tiny keyboard, as Sophia ducked down the first aisle and into the restroom with a relieved sigh.

Was this what her whole trip would be like? Hiding out and doing her best to dodge her past?

The trill of her cell phone offered a welcome distraction, and she reached inside for her purse. When she saw her cousin's number, Sophia winced. Thanks to spotty reception and Theresa's work schedule, they'd been playing phone tag most of the trip. She flipped open the phone, already knowing she was going to get an earful.

"Where are you?" Theresa demanded in place of a normal greeting.

"I'm less than an hour from home," Sophia said as she tucked the phone against her shoulder and turned on the faucet to wash her hands.

"What's happened? What went wrong?"

"*Nothing* went wrong, but thanks for expecting the worst," Sophia said.

"I didn't say *you* did something wrong. But you should have been home by now. We plotted out your route before you left and figured how long it would take."

Theresa had plotted; Sophia had tossed the detailed directions into the back seat where they'd remained. "You also told me to take it easy. No need to hurry, remember?"

"I remember. But at no time did I say to drag your feet the whole way or to delay the inevitable for as long as possible."

Sophia wanted to argue, but her cousin knew her too well.

She glanced at her reflection over the utilitarian sink, seeing her short, dark hair, her brown eyes, the slight upward tilt to her nose. She looked a little pale, a little tired, but nothing out of the ordinary. Nothing hinting at the news she had to share. Still, it was almost like looking into a two-way mirror with Theresa on the other side, seeing all her doubts, her insecurities, her reluctance…

"You have to tell your family the truth."

"I know, Theresa," Sophia said, squelching a touch of irritation. Easy for Theresa to say. She wasn't the one with the big secrets. No, Theresa was the one with the college degree and the good job. But she was also the one who'd welcomed Sophia into her home in St. Louis when she'd been fired by the Dunworthys.

Irritation fading away, Sophia said, "And I would have had to tell them a month ago if you hadn't let me stay with you. If I haven't thanked you for that, I should have. I really appreciate you taking me in for the second time."

Five years ago, when she first left Clearville, she'd gone to live with Theresa in Chicago, where her cousin had been going to college. The move was supposed to be a chance to start over, to wipe the slate clean. For a while, Sophia supposed she'd succeeded, only to mess the whole thing up again, prompting yet another flight to her cousin, who was now living and working in St. Louis.

"You already thanked me, and you know my door is always open. But you can't keep hiding."

"I'm not. I'm going to tell my parents everything." Eventually... Turning away from her reflection, Sophia left the restroom as Theresa pleaded, "Well, at least tell them the truth about Jake Cameron. Every time I talk to my mother, she raves about how handsome and charming he is." Sarcasm coated her words as she affected her mother's husky voice. "She can't stop gloating that she got to be the first one in the family to meet him."

Her cousin's tone softened as she added, "I know how hard it's going to be to tell them all that's happened. And the news about the baby shouldn't be done over the phone. But this stuff with Jake…"

This stuff with Jake… Sophia's heart spasmed at the very mention of his name, and her hand tightened on the phone. She wished she could dismiss Jake Cameron as easily as Theresa had, but Sophia didn't know how she was supposed to do that. Every thought, every memory, every reminder of the time they spent together made it hard to breathe, and yet she couldn't *stop* thinking about him.

Maybe it was an unforeseen drawback of the

years she'd spent as a maid; maybe it was a reaction to the way Todd Dunworthy had treated her and the news of the baby she carried—like dirty secrets to be swept under the carpet. Sophia wasn't sure. All she knew was that the first time Jake smiled at her, the first time he looked at her with those gorgeous, almost golden eyes, she'd felt he could see the *real* Sophia.

Not the Pirellis' little girl. Not the screwup kid sister.

In Jake's eyes, she saw a strong, confident woman reflected back at her. She saw—or she thought she saw—an interest and a desire that made her feel *noticed* for the first time in a long time.

She'd done her best to downplay her feelings for Jake after he left. But what else could she do? Sophia thought. She didn't have any idea how to explain to Theresa her bone-deep certainty that Jake Cameron was a man she could count on, one she could trust, one who would never hurt her. She had yet to figure it out for herself…especially since it turned out none of those things were true.

Once again, she'd trusted the wrong person, only to be let down in the worst possible way.

As for why she hadn't told her family about him, well, that one was a lot easier to understand, Sophia thought as she left the store. Her aunt Donna *had* met Jake when she was visiting from Palm Springs. And Donna had been as charmed as Theresa said. She'd immediately called Clearville, armed with stories about Sophia finally meeting a "nice man."

In truth, Jake Cameron was nothing more than a liar and a fraud, but Aunt Donna didn't know that. She thought he was charming, smart, handsome…

"I just don't get it." Her cousin sucked in a quick breath, then hesitated as if debating what she wanted to say next. "You're not hoping that he'll, I don't know, have some crazy explanation and that you guys can pick up where you left off—"

"No! Of course not. Nothing he could say

would make a bit of difference," she insisted. She hit the button on her keychain remote, the beep of the alarm sounding the exclamation point on her statement.

"Okay. Good." Theresa gave a sigh of relief. "Because that's pretty much what I told him when he called."

"He called?" Sophia demanded, hating the way her heartbeat quickened at the thought. "When?" She slid into the driver's seat, her legs suddenly weak.

After he left St. Louis, Jake had left a few messages. Sophia ignored the calls and they quickly stopped, convincing her she'd done the right thing in refusing to hear out his vague promise of an explanation.

"Yesterday…and maybe a couple of times before that."

"What do you mean, a couple of times?" Sophia asked suspiciously.

"You said you didn't want to talk to him."

"So you didn't bother telling me he called?"

"Would you have called him back?"

"No. Maybe. I don't know. But you didn't have the right to make that decision for me, Theresa."

"I was trying to look out for you. If you didn't want to talk to him—"

"Not the point," Sophia argued. "And by the way, you're really starting to sound like my brothers."

"That's not fair."

Probably not, but this close to home, she was already on the defensive. Despite her poor choices in the present and the past, she needed to prove that she could take care of herself…and the baby she carried.

Taking a breath, she said, "I'm sorry. But if he calls again, let me know, okay? Even if I have no intention of returning his call," she added quickly, then wondered which of them she was trying to convince.

She had no reason to call Jake back. Everything about their relationship had been a lie. So why did she still miss him so much? Why did she still long to hear the sound of his voice?

Because she was an even bigger fool than she

wanted to admit, that was why! Big enough of a fool that she'd daydreamed about how her trip home would be easier with Jake by her side. How his thoughtfulness and charm would impress her mother.… How his wry sense of humor would win over her father.… How his confidence and strength could withstand whatever her some-times obnoxious, oftentimes macho brothers might throw at him.…

"I've always wondered what it would be like to have a big family," he'd told her after listening to one of her childhood memories.

"I'd be happy to share mine," she'd answered, her words not entirely a joke because she'd fooled herself into believing there'd been a yearning hidden in his eyes that might make the impos-sible *possible.*

Her cheeks burned with the memory, but anger served its purpose, withering the unwanted seeds of hope that blossomed inside her simply because he'd called a few times.

"All right. I'll let you know if he calls again," her cousin said, grudgingly enough to tell Sophia her feelings were still hurt. "I have to work tonight, but leave me a message when you get to Clearville."

As she dropped her phone back in her purse, Sophia admitted she really shouldn't have jumped on Theresa for keeping secrets. Not when she had so many of her own.

And certainly not when she wasn't planning to come clean on all of them. Oh, she'd tell her family about losing her job in Chicago. And of course, she would tell them about the pregnancy. But about Jake—the truth about Jake Cameron was one secret Sophia planned on keeping.

Yes, he was a liar and a total jerk. But that didn't really matter.

All that mattered was that her aunt had met Jake. She thought he was a nice guy. So who did it hurt if her family believed they were still dating? If her family thought, maybe, they were even falling in love? Was it really so bad of her to want to have one bright spot to point to? A single light at the end of the tunnel?

No one needed to know she'd already been run over by the train.

After the long, drawn-out days of traveling—Theresa had been right to accuse her of dragging her feet—Sophia should have been eager to have the trip behind her. She should have been grateful to escape her tiny cramped car; she should have longed for a half-hour soak in a tub instead of a five-minute shower with limited heat and water pressure; she should have been looking forward to spending the night in a comfortable, familiar bed.

She would find all of that at her parents' house, and yet she dreaded seeing her family, fielding all their questions and admitting to a truth that made her feel so, so stupid.

It would have been bad enough if she were the only one affected, but she wasn't. The child she carried would have to live with it as well, and the questions she dreaded her family asking would be nothing compared to those her child might ask six or seven years down the road.

So maybe she could use this trip as something of a test drive, a practice run long before she had to tell her child.

Pulling up to her parents' sprawling white-sided farmhouse with its green shutters and wraparound front porch, Sophia cut the engine and took a deep breath. The house showed signs of a facelift. Nothing dramatic, but Sophia could see the paint was new, the old wrought iron railing had been replaced by a white wooden picket fence, and the stairs leading to the porch no longer sagged in the middle. Terra cotta flower pots filled with petunias, snapdragons and vinca lined the steps in welcome, and the huge, green lawn stretched out on either side of the house before giving way to uncultivated wilderness.

She could think of dozens of descriptions, but only one word came to mind.

Home.

"Here we go, baby."

She patted her tummy, then grabbed her purse and climbed from the car, leaving her suitcases behind in the trunk. Big, burly brothers were good for a few things, after all. And Sophia didn't doubt her brothers would be at the house. Sunday night dinners were legendary in the Pirelli household. Her mother always made enough food to feed an army. And over the years, between her brothers' friends, girlfriends and later, at least in Nick's case, family, an army of guests had frequently shown up, often out of the blue.

And Vanessa Pirelli always greeted her guests—expected or not—with a smile and a homemade meal.

"Spaghetti," Sophia whispered as she walked toward the front door. "Please be having spaghetti."

Not only because she'd missed her mother's spaghetti, unable to imitate the handed-down family recipe no matter how many times she tried, but because the meal was her brothers' favorite. Her mother often joked that a bomb could go off, and none of them would drop a fork.

Sophia hoped her mother was right, and she could drop a couple of *her* bombs without her brothers going ballistic. *Sam, any chance you'll save some meatballs for the rest of us...and oh, by the way, I was fired from my job. Drew, pass the milk, will you? I'm supposed to get more calcium, being pregnant and all.*

And her parents...she could already imagine the disappointment in their eyes.

Her insides churning, her steps had slowed to a shuffle as she crossed the porch. The hoped-for aroma of simmering tomato sauce and garlic bread didn't immediately tease her senses as she opened the front door and stepped inside. Sophia sniffed, but she couldn't smell anything cooking at all. Nor did she hear the usual sounds of a Pirelli dinner, the clink of glasses, the scrape of silverware against china, the arguments between Nick and Drew over sports, the arguments between Sam and everyone over anything.

The updates to the outside of the house continued inside. The hardwood floors gleamed beneath a new coat of stain and faintly striped wallpaper brought out the floral patterns in the chintz sofa and armchairs. But the focal point of the room, a family portrait hanging above the red brick fireplace mantel, remained.

Taken several years ago, the portrait showed her three brothers in back. Nick, the oldest, was in the middle, flanked on either side by Drew, who shared Nick's dark coloring, and by Sam, the only blond-haired one in the bunch. Her parents were seated in front of the boys—her father, an older, leaner version of his sons, his thick dark hair sprinkled with gray and laugh lines around his dark-brown eyes, and her mother, as petite as her husband and sons were tall, her chestnut hair cut in a sleek bob to frame her round face and green eyes. Sophia sat front and center, her dark hair longer back then, smiling at the camera with all the confidence of an eighteen-year-old kid ready to conquer the world.

Sophia sighed. Little had she known.

Walking toward the back of the house, she expected to find some member of her family—her parents would never dream of eating out on a Sunday night. But the comfortable kitchen, with its oak cabinets, matching table and chairs and green gingham accents, was empty.

Sophia turned in a circle, feeling somewhat lost in her childhood home, until the sound of laughter rang in the distance. With a glance at the back door, she smiled despite the churning in her stomach. Of course. The weather was perfect for a barbecue, and grilling outdoors was the one chance her mother had in getting someone else to cook a meal.

Plastering on a smile, Sophia opened the back door and stepped out onto the porch. "Hey, everybody, I'm home," she announced, preparing for the usual enthusiastic greetings that never failed to disguise the worry and question in her family's eyes.

Shouts of "Sweetheart!" "Squirt!" and "Fifi!" rang out, the last despised nickname coming from Sam, who called her that only to annoy her.

But one voice she never expected to hear spoke quietly in her ear. "Hello, Sophia."

Speechless, she turned and gazed into Jake Cameron's amber eyes.

Chapter Two

Jake Cameron. Here. At her parents' house.
With her family. Wearing—was that her mother's apron? Sophia blinked hard, twice, but when
she opened her eyes, Jake still stood mere inches
away, his expression serious despite the frilly
white apron covered by pink potbellied pigs.

She was dreaming. Her foolish, foolish wish of
having Jake accompany her to her parents' house
had slipped into her subconscious, where she
was too vulnerable to keep the ridiculous hope at
bay. That was the only possible explanation. She
was still asleep at some by-the-highway hotel,

her face smashed into a cheap pillow, having a doozy of a nightmare. The breeze carried the scent of charcoal and the sounds of her family's greetings, but none of it was real.

Jake even looked as he always did in her dreams—too tempting for her peace of mind and too good to be true, she thought, her hungry gaze taking in rugged features that had become breathtakingly familiar in such a short time. The setting sun burnished his brown hair, bringing out the highlights in the slightly shaggy strands, and turning his skin to gold. Faint lines fanned out from his whiskey-colored eyes, hinting at a smile that could flash lightning quick or start her body on a slow burn with sexy, seductive deliberation.

If she closed her eyes, she could still feel the heated promise of his lips against hers in intoxicating kisses that made her forget the harsh lessons of the past. But she didn't need to close her eyes because she was already asleep. Sophia was sure of it…

Until Jake reached out, trailed his fingers down

the all-too-sensitive inside of her arm and took her hand. Her heart slammed in her chest, hard enough to stop its beat and steal her breath, and Sophia knew this was happening, this was real. Because nothing—not a dream, not a nightmare, not a figment of her imagination—could affect her like this.

Nothing but living, breathing, flesh-and-blood Jake Cameron could make her feel this way.

Sophia jerked her hand from his as she choked out in a whisper, "What—what are you doing here?"

Before Jake had the chance to answer, Sam bounded up the back steps to the small landing. "We didn't know you'd be bringing company, but hey! More the merrier!" Sam slapped Jake on the back hard enough to knock a smaller man aside, but Jake absorbed the blow with little re-action. Her brother dropped a kiss on her cheek as he brushed by. "Good to see you, Fifi. And about time, too."

Sophia could barely manage a response to her brother's greeting. She'd imagined dozens of scenarios where she had a chance to confront Jake Cameron and let him have it for lying to her. In those somewhat vengeful daydreams, she was sharp, clever and cutting enough to bring him to his knees. Never, though, in any of those scenes had she pictured a moment like this.

"Let me guess," she said, a hint of hysteria creeping into her voice, "the apron was Sam's idea."

Jake glanced down at the parade of pigs. "He said it was the only one." His knowing look told Sophia he hadn't believed it for a second, but then again—

"Takes one to know one," she muttered beneath her breath, but not so quietly that Jake didn't still hear, judging by the muscle tightening in his jaw.

As the screen door slammed shut behind Sam, Sophia gradually became aware of the rest of her family. Nick and Drew had apparently been in the middle of a supposedly touch football game, judging by the grass stains on Drew's jeans and the ball tucked beneath Nick's arm. Her father stood at the grill Jake had abandoned and her mother and Nick's daughter, Maddie, had been sitting beneath the gazebo off to the side of the yard.

At Sophia's arrival, though, everyone charged en masse, giving Jake little time to reply and Sophia less time to prepare. She'd barely made it down the back steps when her mother and niece reached her, Vanessa hugging her shoulders while seven-year-old Maddie wrapped her skinny arms around her waist. "Sophia! It's so good to see you. I've missed you."

Wrapped in a cloud of cinnamon-scented warmth, Sophia swallowed hard. "Missed you too, Mom."

Vanessa Pirelli pulled back, her green eyes taking quick inventory of her only daughter. Sophia instinctively stiffened as she waited for the questions to cloud her mother's expression with worry. *Was she okay? Was she in trouble? Had she fallen in with the wrong crowd again?*

To Sophia's surprise, and for the first time in years, disappointment failed to dim the light in her mother's eyes. Not until her mother included Jake in her happy gaze did Sophia fully understand why. "Wasn't it sweet of Jake to surprise you like this?"

"It's a surprise," she agreed, avoiding the "sweet" description when it came to Jake Cameron.

Her fault, of course, for letting the deception go on as long as she had. Was there some ugly, painful stone in her dismal love life he'd somehow left unturned? He was headed for disappointment. She'd spilled her heart to him already.

She'd foolishly felt she *owed* him the truth—that she was being unfair to start any kind of relationship without telling Jake about the child she carried. Turned out she didn't owe him at all. He was already getting paid, and how unfair was that?

She felt Jake's intense gaze on the side of her face, as if his golden eyes gave off as much heat as the man himself, but she refused to glance his way. Struggling for normalcy in front of her family, Sophia focused on her niece. She cupped the girl's dimpled chin in her hand and exclaimed, "Maddie, I think you've grown a foot since I saw you last!"

"I'm starting third grade soon! I'll be in Mrs. Dawson's class," the tiny, girlish version of her big brother said, her whole body practically vibrating with excitement. In Clearville's small elementary school, first and second grades were housed together in the same classroom. Entering third grade was an enormous step.

"You're one of the big kids now!" Sophia exclaimed. "Practically all grown up!"

"It's amazing how fast kids change when you aren't around to see it," Nick drawled, shifting the football to his other hand to draw his daughter to his side.

Sophia had to give him credit; she might have actually believed the casual comment was nothing more than that if she didn't know better. But she did. Her oldest brother still blamed her for taking off to Chicago and for the fallout she hadn't intended to cause.

But any defense Sophia might have made

collapsed at the combination of love, pride and well-disguised worry that mingled in his gaze as he looked down at his daughter. "She'll be in college before I know it."

Sophia's heart clenched in sympathy for what Nick had gone through since his wife left, in guilt for her part in Carol's desertion, and in a newly realized panic knowing she'd be feeling that same love, that same pride, that same worry soon for her own child. Like Nick, she too would be alone.

Sophia swallowed hard, and it had to be her imagination that Jake stepped closer as if sensing her thoughts and offering his silent support.

Crazy, she thought. If Jake could read her mind, he'd run the other way. Because she was still mad at him. Really, really mad.

Mad enough to haul off and hit him. Mad enough to throw herself into his arms, close her eyes, and pretend the Jake Cameron she'd met in St. Louis was the *real* Jake Cameron…

"Hey, Jake!" Her dad waved a barbecue fork in

their direction. "How 'bout you take over here and give me a chance to hug my little girl?"

"You got it, Vince. Be right there."

Trying to keep her jaw from dropping at the warm welcome embracing Jake, Sophia shot him a sidelong glance he caught front and center. He stepped closer until she had to tilt her head back to meet his gaze. She'd lived with older and much taller brothers her entire life; she was used to their overwhelming breadth and height.

But with Jake, it was…different.

Intimidating and at the same time thrilling in ways she wished she could forget.

"I've missed you," he murmured, his deep voice tripping over nerve endings and raising goose bumps across her skin.

Fury at her reaction as much as at his words reared, and Sophia sucked in a breath, sharp retort at the ready. But before she could say a single word, Jake caught the back of her neck, his fingers tunneling in her dark hair, and pulled her into a quick, hard kiss.

She barely had the chance to register his taste,

to respond to the press of his mouth against hers, to relive the memory of the kisses they'd shared in St. Louis. Kisses that slipped beneath her defenses, exploited her weaknesses…

She drew in a second breath as she pulled back, still ready to blast him with her temper, still furious, but Jake had already stepped away.

"Jake, I can't tell you what a pleasure it is to have you here." Vanessa Pirelli's warm smile left no room to doubt the sincerity of her words.

Seated across from Sophia's mother, Jake worked on a smile of his own. The casual meal around the picnic table was nothing like the formal family dinners in the Cameron household. Her welcoming acceptance should have made it easier, but the whole experience of holding hands while saying grace, passing rolls across the table like lobbing softballs and carrying on four conversations at one time seemed like something out of a storybook.

And of course every story had its villain, a role Jake had been fully willing to accept when he showed up unannounced at Sophia's home. But instead of hurling accusations, her family had greeted him with open arms—literally—leaving him feeling off-balance and unprepared. He'd been ready to face the Pirelli family's anger; their approval was unexpected…and unde-served.

Still, he said, "I'm glad to be here, Mrs. Pi-relli."

Glad to see for himself that Sophia had a family who loved her, who would be there for her and her child in a way only family *could* be. She might not have told them about the baby yet, but it was obvious Sophia's child would have three doting uncles and one set of grandparents to spoil him rotten and to be there for anything he needed.

"Oh, now, didn't I tell you to call me Vanessa?" Sophia's mother reminded him.

"Yes, ma'am, you did."

His evasion didn't get by the older woman, and her eyes crinkled in a smile, small lines forming at the corners, giving him a glimpse

of how beautiful Sophia would look as she ma-
tured. Only Sophia certainly wasn't smiling at
him now.

Sitting stiff and silent at his side, Sophia's
body language told him loud and clear she didn't
share in her mother's welcome. But not even her
anger and the obvious emotional walls stopped
him from noticing the way her dark hair curled
behind her ear to perfectly frame her delicate
features. Or the way the afternoon breeze picked
up the fresh vanilla scent of her skin. Or the heat
of her body inches from his.

When she reached out to pass the potato salad
and brushed her arm against his, every hair on
his body seemed to stand at attention—thousands of tiny divining rods guiding him to the
woman at his side. A woman he'd told himself
a hundred times since leaving St. Louis he was
better off staying away from. Yet here he was,
sitting by her side like a man who'd been out in
the desert too long and yet somehow thought he
could ignore the temptation of taking a drink.

He hadn't even made it five minutes before

kissing her, Jake thought wryly, unable to resist putting his memory to the test to see if Sophia's lips truly were as sweet and soft as he recalled. Even that brief taste told him what he'd already come to suspect in the days since he left St. Louis: memories were no substitute for the real thing. The real thing he'd found in Sophia…

Jake shoved the thought aside. He wasn't some starry-eyed romantic. He didn't believe in love at first sight. He wasn't sure he believed in love at all.

His only experience with the painful emotion had been Mollie. At the time, he'd certainly thought he loved her and trusted she felt the same. But that day at the hospital, she'd made it more than clear how she really felt about him.

You aren't a family man, Jake. You don't have any idea what it's like to be part of a family, but that's what I need. That's what Josh and I both need.

And that was what Sophia needed, too.

She needed her family to rally around her, and if playing her boyfriend made this reunion a little easier on her, well, he could fill in for now. He could take on the part until she found someone better suited. Much like Mollie had.

Slipping back into a role that had become too familiar too fast in St. Louis, Jake returned Vanessa's smile. "Sophia's told me so much about you, and I couldn't wait to meet you all."

"You'll have to make sure Sophia shows you around while she's here. Last time she was home, she didn't do much more than hide away in her room."

"Sam!" his mother admonished, but whatever the reason for the sudden silence that fell over the table, Sam seemed as ignorant of its cause as Jake.

"What?" the youngest of the Pirelli brothers asked. "I'm just saying."

"Can you blame her?" Drew slugged his younger brother on the shoulder. "She was probably hiding out from you."

Jake had already figured out that Sam was the joker, Drew something of a peacemaker, while Nick—Nick he had yet to figure out. The eldest

Pirelli brother obviously adored his daughter and got along well with the rest of his family, but Jake sensed a tension between Nick and Sophia, a distance the family clearly talked around, as they did the absence of Maddie's mother.

"So, Jake, what is it you do?" Sophia's father asked as he dug in to the potato salad.

He knew from what Sophia had told him that Nick was a veterinarian, Drew a custom-home builder and Sam a mechanic. But Jake didn't know *what* she'd told her family about him.

Buying some time, he took a huge bite of the hamburger he'd piled high with lettuce, cheese, avocado and tomatoes. The flavors exploded against his tongue, tasting better than anything he'd had to eat since—since the last meal he shared with Sophia.

They'd gone to a barbecue place not far from her cousin's house. It had been the final time Sophia looked at him without suspicion, anger and distrust filling her expression. He'd told her the truth the next day, but he had no idea if she'd told her family about his occupation.

Unfortunately, Sophia didn't seem the least bit inclined to jump in and save him. She was focused on her own burger, sans any toppings, a preference he remembered from a hot dog she'd ordered at a Cardinals game. Almost embarrassed, she'd confessed, "What can I say? I have boring tastes."

Jake hadn't found anything at all boring about Sophia Pirelli, and he'd declared her a hot dog purist. Laughing in response, she'd comically piled every condiment known to man on the hot dog he'd purchased while he made a big deal about covering hers with a napkin to maintain its pristine, natural state...

"Um, Jake," Sophia finally prompted. "My dad was asking about your job."

"Yeah, sorry about that." Jake swallowed the last of the huge bite he'd taken. "My mother would be appalled by my manners."

"Mom's always appalled by our manners," Sam interjected, clearly unconcerned as he grabbed a cherry tomato from the salad bowl and popped it into his mouth.

Vanessa rolled her eyes. "Isn't that the truth?"

"Anyway," Jake began after he'd stalled as long as he could and hoping he'd picked up correctly on the slight disapproval in Sophia's voice when she mentioned his job. "I'm a private investigator."

"Seriously? That must be *so* cool," Sam declared.

"Yes, Jake, tell Sam how *cool* your job is," Sophia said, a challenging lift to her eyebrows.

He was still scrambling for something to say that would appease her brothers' curiosity without further alienating Sophia when Vince asked his daughter, "Why is now the first we're hearing of this? Sophia, why didn't you tell us what Jake does for a living? For all we knew, he could have been an accountant."

Sophia picked at the sesame seeds on her hamburger bun and complained, "What's wrong with being an accountant?"

"Other than being totally boring?" Sam asked before turning back to Jake. "What was your most interesting case?"

Jake didn't have to even think about it. "That would have to be the case that took me to St. Louis."

Sophia's head snapped toward him, her dark gaze pleading, as if she expected him to blurt out the whole story to her family right there at the dinner table. Any why not? he thought with regret. That was pretty much what he'd done to her...

Sam leaned forward. "What happened in St. Louis?"

Reaching out, Jake lifted Sophia's hand from the picnic table and entwined her fingers with his own. "That's where I met your sister," he murmured.

The worry eased from her expression, and was it his imagination or had her eyes softened just a little? Despite the elbow-to-elbow contact at the table, her family seemed to fade away, leaving just the two of them and the spark that had ignited between them the moment they met, an attraction that made it easy for Sophia to trust him, an attraction that made it so easy for Jake to lie to her.

He didn't know which of them flinched first, but the break in contact as Sophia's hand fell to her side made Jake feel like some vital part of him had been ripped away, leaving behind only scars as reminders of all he'd lost. Because of his lies and because of the truth he'd been asked to find.

Dammit, Sophia, I'm sorry, he thought, staring at her downcast profile as if he might will her into accepting his apology. *Sorry I'm not the man you thought I was.*

He did his best to deflect the rest of her family's questions about his job and thought he'd just about turned the tide when Maddie's young voice piped in.

"Have you ever been shot?"

The little girl had been tossing bits of her bun at a couple of birds, and Jake hadn't thought she'd been listening to the conversation. When all adult eyes focused on her, she added, "You know, like on TV."

Instinctively, his hand moved to his left thigh. Sometimes he swore he could still feel the bullet burning beneath his flesh even though he knew that was impossible…. A soft intake of breath beside him caught his attention. Sophia straightened in realization, and he could almost hear yet another mark checked off against him for yet another lie.

He was spared from having to satisfy Maddie's childish curiosity when Vanessa turned on her eldest son. "Honestly, Nick, what have you been letting this child watch?"

"I didn't *let* her. I didn't know she was paying any attention," Nick protested.

Thinking it was a good time to turn the conversation away from himself while he still could, Jake asked, "What about you, Vince? What do you do?"

For the first time since he met the Pirelli family, silence fell.

Sophia might not think much of Jake's job, but up until recently, he'd been good at it. And he could still pick up on body language and small

nuances most people missed. Like the encouraging smile Vanessa sent her husband's way. Like
the look Sam and Drew exchanged, and Nick's
brief but pointed glance at Sophia, who kept her
own eyes focused on her plate. Only Maddie was
immune, singing beneath her breath and turning
her attention back to her gathering flock.

Vince's smile was wide as ever, but something
less than genuine as he said, "Used to manage
the grocery store in town, but now I'm retired.
I get to be a full-time husband and father, much
to my wife and kids' dismay."

Vanessa and his sons immediately protested,
but Sophia stayed stone silent at Jake's side until
she stood abruptly and practically scrambled
over the picnic bench. She grabbed her glass
of lemonade. "I need a refill. I'll be right back.
Can I get anyone anything from the kitchen?"
She barely waited for her family to reply before
backing away from the table.

Jake stood before she made her escape. "I'll
join you."

She opened her mouth to demur, but he shot

a quick glance at her family and the protest she would have made transformed into a smile. "Thank you, Jake."

"You're welcome," he said, wondering if he was the only one to notice how she spoke the words through gritted teeth.

He caught her hand as they crossed the lush green lawn toward the kitchen, but it was Sophia who practically dragged him the last few yards into the house. She whirled on him the moment the door closed, secluding them in the homey kitchen.

Her color was high and her dark eyes snapping as she bit out, "Football injury?"

"What?"

"The night we met, you said you were limping because of a football injury!"

Of all the explanations he owed Sophia, that was by far the last he'd expected her to demand. He'd passed off his injury with the half-joking cliché rather than tell the truth. But the worry shining through her anger was far worse than facing the memories of the job that had gone wrong in Mexico only a few weeks before he met Sophia.

"I wasn't lying when I told you I was fine. I am," he insisted, wondering if he wasn't trying to convince himself. Physically, yes, he was healing. But how many times had he awakened in a cold sweat, grabbing at his leg, feeling the pain of the bullet buried deep inside? He thought he'd put those nightmares to rest, but they'd come back with a vengeance since he left St. Louis. Since he'd left Sophia.

She stared up at him as if trying to see right through him and straight into all the uncertainty inside. But he'd gotten good over the years at hiding; it was part of his job, sure, but more than that, it was part of who he was. And he was pretty sure he didn't give anything away when he repeated, "I'm fine."

For a moment, she looked ready to argue, the fine line between her eyebrows a dead giveaway of the stubbornness he'd caught a glimpse of a time or two in St. Louis. But then she changed tactics as she got to the point. "What are you doing here, Jake?"

He'd asked that question as he traveled to Clearville and still wasn't sure he'd come up with an adequate answer to satisfy himself, let alone one Sophia would accept. All he knew was that the hurt in her eyes when he'd blurted out the truth had haunted him since he'd left, and he couldn't stand the thought of that being his last memory of Sophia. So here he was, standing in the kitchen of her childhood home, ready to give an explanation she didn't want to hear. An apology she wouldn't accept.

Her crossed arms, raised chin and closed expression all told him she wasn't going to listen to anything he had to say. Not here, not now. But he had time…if he dared to take it.

"What am I doing?" he echoed. "I'm enjoying your family's company. I'd expected I'd have to fight through your brothers to see you—" his eyebrow rose in question "—but for some crazy reason, they think we're dating."

Evading his gaze, she focused on a wall clock

shaped like a rooster. Color slowly faded from her cheeks, along with her previous fire, and Jake dropped any hint of teasing. "What's going on, Sophia?"

She shook her head and swallowed. "It's like you said. My family still thinks we're dating... for the crazy reason that I haven't told them otherwise."

"Just like you haven't told them what happened in Chicago or that you're no longer working for the Dunworthys." From what he gathered in passing conversations, her family had no idea Sophia had been fired...or the reason why. The Pirellis seemed to think Sophia was on paid leave while her employers vacationed overseas.

"Yet another proud moment in my life," she muttered. Her embarrassment and disappointment was obvious in the slump to her shoulders and downcast eyes. Jake felt his heart lurch as if urging him to do something. Uncertain what else he could offer, he quietly asked, "Do you want me to tell your family what happened?"

Dragging her gaze from the ceramic tile that

had replaced the worn linoleum floor of her childhood, Sophia stared up at Jake Cameron, a man who knew the worst and best of the secrets she still hadn't told her family. A man who was a virtual stranger—since for all she knew everything he'd told her was a lie, a man who treated getting *shot* like a paper cut—and the urge to escape overwhelmed her. She spun toward the door, but her family still waited outside. The trapped, suffocating feeling she'd had as a teenager closed in on her, reminding her of all the reasons why she'd run from Clearville years ago.

But a different edge raced along the fine blade of tension now, one she'd never felt before meeting Jake. A fear that running would never be enough until she found some place—someone—she could run to. She shoved the ridiculous thought aside and took a deep breath that teased her senses with the hint of Jake's woodsy aftershave combined with the smoke from the charcoal—a scent more appetizing than the burgers he'd grilled.

"Do you want me to?" he asked again, stepping

close enough for her to feel the heat of his body running down her spine, buttocks and the backs of her thighs. She turned to face him, realizing too late the temptation of his broad chest was just a deep breath away from her breasts and his lips hovered just out of reach of her own… unless she stood on tiptoe, as she'd learned the night of their second date.

"Sophia?"

"What?" Sophia demanded, horrified she'd somehow given her desire away.

"Do you want me to tell your family?" he repeated, a slight frown coming to his handsome face.

Feeling her cheeks burn, she shook her head to clear her heated thoughts. "Of course not," she scoffed, though she was a bit tempted to dump all the responsibility on Jake. But she wasn't *that* big of a coward. "They're my family. I'll tell them."

His golden gaze searched hers, his expression more enigmatic than she'd ever seen in St. Louis. For those few short weeks, he'd struck her as completely sincere, honest and easy to read. It hurt all over again to realize not only his words had been a lie. Everything about the Jake Cameron she'd met, the Jake Cameron she'd *liked* had been a con.

"Or…" His voice trailed off, dangling the bait of an answer she had yet to consider.

"Or what?"

"Or you could let them believe we're still seeing each other until you're ready to tell the truth."

That had been her plan all along, hadn't it? Easing into the truth like dipping a toe into the shock of an icy pond instead of diving in headlong. But looking up into the intensity of Jake's golden gaze, she felt the heat of his stare searching her face before settling on her mouth. A sudden trembling attacked her legs and threatened her ability to stand. Desperate to fight off that weakness before Jake could see how easily he still affected her, Sophia mocked, "You mean *pretend* to be dating? Well, *you'd* certainly be good at it."

His jaw tightened to the point where she expected to hear his molars crack, but when he spoke, his voice was as deep and calm as ever. "You have a choice, Sophia."

His gaze shifted to a spot over her shoulder, and she glanced back. The lace curtain over the back door window offered a snowy, diffused view of her family outside. Sam and Drew were telling some story that had both her parents laughing. Even Nick looked like he was enjoying himself.

Once again, she would be the one changing that, wiping away their happiness and replacing it with worry and disappointment. Swallowing, she turned away and looked back at Jake. "Why would you do this?"

"Let's just say I owe you," he said. "There is a condition, though."

"Figures," she muttered. "What's the condition?"

"I want to know why you've let your family believe we're still seeing each other."

Tell Jake or tell her entire family? Math had

never been her favorite subject, but even she could do those calculations. "You remember meeting my aunt Donna when she came to visit Theresa?" At Jake's nod, Sophia said, "Well, she definitely remembers meeting you. All she could talk about was what a great guy you are."

Jake flinched at her words, and for the first time, Sophia wondered if his guilt and regret might be the real thing.

That, or he's playing you, a cynical voice warned. *The same way he played you from the moment you met...or maybe even before that.*

It wasn't like her to view every action with suspicion and doubt, but she'd been burned too many times before. If she let herself believe anything Jake said, she'd only be setting herself up for another heartache.

"Sophia—"

She shook her head, cutting off an apology she couldn't afford to accept. "My parents have been married for thirty-five years. I know how rare that is in this day and age, but in my family, people still believe that's the way it's supposed to be. That marriage is for life and family means everything. How am I supposed to admit that I'm pregnant and that the father of my child will always be this nameless, faceless nonentity in our lives? In my child's life?"

Sophia didn't mean for the words to keep spilling out, but once she started, she couldn't seem to stop. "But you! See, my aunt Donna met you! She thought you were a nice guy. I even had a few pictures from when we went out—to the ballgame, and the zoo." Sophia shook her head. "You were a single bright spot amid everything that was going wrong in my life and—it was stupid to think that would be enough. But, I don't know, it just seemed like better than nothing."

Her hands dropped uselessly to her sides, and she glanced up at Jake, anticipating his reaction. What she saw, though, was the last thing she expected. Tension had taken hold of his body, leaving behind taut lines of muscle and bone. "Jake—"

The back door opened before she could say anything more. Sam bounded inside, nearly running her down. "Sorry, sis," he said as he caught her by the shoulders and steered her out of the way. Breaking up the tense moment with typical oblivion, he headed for the refrigerator. "Maddie says there's cake for dessert."

Her mother followed a moment later. Far more perceptive than Sam—but who wasn't?—she looked back and forth between Sophia and Jake. "Is everything all right?"

Jake gave an abrupt nod as he escaped from the kitchen. Meeting her mother's puzzled look, Sophia forced a smile and said, "I'm, um, a little tired from the trip. I'd like to go lie down for awhile."

"Oh, of course. Are your bags still in the car?"

"In the trunk," she said.

"Sam, go get your sister's luggage when you're done in here."

Backing out of the refrigerator with the sheet cake, Sam said, "Will do."

Her mother linked her arm through Sophia's. "Your room is ready. If you need anything—

well," she said with a smile, "you probably know where it is."

The house where she'd grown up hadn't changed that much over the years, and Sophia shouldn't have been surprised when her mother opened the door to her bedroom. Stuck in a time warp from Sophia's late teens, the room looked exactly as it had when she left. Same white wrought-iron day bed. Same rainbow of accent colors since she'd never been able to settle on just one or two—the candy-striped pink and white wallpaper, the lilac shag area rug, the powder-blue comforter and vast array of throw pillows. She'd painted the furniture herself, taking the dresser and nightstand from plain white to wild mixes of polka dots, stripes, hearts and flowers.

Seeing it all, Sophia couldn't speak around the lump in her throat, but there was so much she wanted to say, so many explanations, so many apologies…

But Vanessa said the only words that mattered. "We've missed you, sweetheart. I'm so glad you're home."

Surrounded by her childhood things and the unconditional love shining in her mother's eyes, the truth about the baby, about her job, about Jake bubbled up. "Mom—"

"I see you still haven't learned to pack light," Sam remarked as he shouldered his way into the room, two suitcases in hand and one tucked beneath his arm like a football.

The opportunity to tell the truth dissipated like smoke, leaving behind only a hint of the chance she'd let slip by, and Sophia forced a smile at her brother. She'd brought almost everything she owned, unsure from day to day what clothes would still fit over her gradually expanding belly.

As soon as Sam swung the suitcases onto the bed, Vanessa said, "And let Jake know his room is ready, too, would you?"

Sophia froze in shock. "Jake? Jake's staying here?"

"Well, of course, dear," her mother said with a frown. "You didn't think we'd expect him to take a room in town, did you?"

Sophia swallowed a lump of nerves. Keeping up the charade might have been Jake's idea, but she'd agreed to it, hadn't she? A pretend boyfriend was one thing. But how on earth was she supposed to handle the real Jake Cameron sleeping under the same roof only a few doors away?

Chapter Three

Why would you do this?

Jake's hands tightened on the back porch railing as Sophia's words echoed through his thoughts. He wondered what her reaction would have been if he'd told her the truth.

He missed her. He missed her laughter, her smile, and that he'd considered admitting that, even for a split second, told Jake he was already in over his head.

He'd made the biggest mistake an investigator could—he'd gotten too close to the subject. He knew better than to let emotions rule his actions.

Logic and patience and detached observation had made him a good private investigator, but for the second job in a row, he'd rushed in without thinking. His body was still healing from the painful lessons he'd learned in Mexico while the damage done in St. Louis…those wounds were harder to define, but they'd left him reeling. Especially since he still didn't know how Sophia had sneaked past his defenses.

Was it the evening they'd ended up missing their dinner reservation when she saw a small school carnival and wanted to stop? How she'd egged him on as he spent over twenty bucks popping balloons to win her a palm-sized stuffed unicorn? Was it the Cardinals game they went to and the thirty-minute rain delay they spent huddled beneath a shared umbrella, talking and laughing? Normal, everyday activities that made life—made *him*—feel normal again…

Or had it happened so much sooner than that? The night they first met, when he'd wrestled her bag away from a purse snatcher. He'd ended up with some scrapes on his hand, minor cuts

Sophia had insisted on bandaging. The scratches had long since healed, but the soft brush of her skin against his lingered…

Jake let go of the railing and shoved his hands into his back pockets. It didn't really matter how or when it had happened. Only that he couldn't let Sophia crawl any deeper into his heart.

When Sophia told him she was pregnant with Todd Dunworthy's child, Jake had felt like the cruel hand of fate was trying to shove him down a rocky, heaving path, but it was a road he refused to go down again. He wouldn't. He *couldn't.*

Even as he'd listened to Sophia talk about the father of her child—a nameless, faceless nonentity—unwanted memories of Mollie and Josh had crept in. Regret and failure clenched at his gut. It was enough to make Jake feel like *less* than nothing. Which was exactly what he'd ended up being to Josh despite his best attempts.

The back door opened behind him, and Sam said, "Hey, we've got dessert ready if Drew and Nick didn't already eat it all."

He wasn't in the mood to eat or even to join the Pirelli family without Sophia at the table. He was glad when Sam added, "And my mom wanted me to tell you your room's ready if you want to bring your stuff in from the car."

The elder Pirellis had made the offer as soon as he arrived, but he'd expected to leave once Sophia showed up. Now, though, he forced himself to accept that he was going to stay. He owed this to Sophia.

If his presence made it easier for her to tell her parents about the baby, then he could stay a day or two. Just to make sure everything was all right and that Sophia was once again safely ensconced in the heart of her family.

After several sleepless nights leading up to her trip home, not to mention tossing and turning in unfamiliar hotel beds while on the road, Sophia expected to curl up into her old twin bed and fall asleep the second her head hit the floral-patterned pillow.

Instead, she found herself staring at the ceiling.

Even her recent, slightly silly habit of singing lullabies beneath her breath to her unborn baby hadn't relaxed her. The excitement of the day had simply caught up with her; little wonder she couldn't sleep.

And Jake Cameron lying in bed down the hall has nothing to do with it, her conscience mocked.

"Oh, hush," she muttered to the voice that hadn't stopped harping at her all evening. Tossing aside the covers, she decided a glass of warm milk would be just the thing to quiet the annoying voice and send her right to sleep.

She'd never cared much for milk, but Theresa had frequently pressed a cold glass or warm mug into her hand. "Milk," her cousin quipped, "it does a baby good."

And Sophia was willing to do whatever it took to keep her baby healthy and happy.

A nightlight in the hall lit the way to the kitchen. She could have made it in total darkness, and Sophia had to admit the familiarity gave her a sense of comfort she hadn't felt in years. But the feeling disappeared as she hurried by the closed guest room door.

She didn't need to think about Jake sprawled out across a queen bed that was likely too short for his long, lean frame...

Banishing the image from her mind, she rushed toward the kitchen, making a beeline for the fridge. Blinking against the light spilling out as she opened the door, she reached for the half-gallon container.

"Can't sleep?"

Sophia gasped at the unexpected sound of a deep voice behind her. She spun around and for the first time noticed a dark shadow at the table. He still wore the jeans and T-shirt from earlier, and Sophia wondered how long he'd been sitting there. Her heart picked up its pace as Jake stood and crossed the small kitchen to stand in front of her. The single bulb that had seemed bright before now shone like a spotlight, emphasizing his tousled dark-blond hair, the rough stubble grazing his jaw, and she couldn't look away.

With the heat coming off Jake's body and the

refrigerated air at her back, Sophia half expected a spontaneous tornado to sweep through the kitchen—a storm certainly seemed to be brewing inside her.

"Sophia." His voice held a hint of warning, and her gaze instantly rose to meet his. The desire she saw there only amplified the longing spinning through her in ever tightening circles, spiraling down into a pinpoint focus. She wanted him to kiss her. To let the heat and urgency of his mouth against hers wipe away the past weeks. To turn back time to those few, short days when Jake Cameron was a man she could trust, a man she could count on…

Instead of a man who lied.

Realization hitting with an embarrassment that Jake could so easily turn her on even though he *had* lied, Sophia spun back toward the fridge.

"Uh, no. I couldn't sleep." She busied herself with taking out the milk, wishing she could press the cold container against her heated face. "I thought some warm milk might help. I can fix you some if you'd like."

"I don't think warm milk will do the trick."

As the refrigerator door swung shut, the kitchen was once again wrapped in semi-darkness. Just as well, since Sophia feared seeing more in Jake's expression than she wanted to know. She found a small saucepan right where it had always been and set it on the stove. "You know, just because we're pretending to be dating doesn't mean you have to stay. You could say something came up with work."

"What kind of boyfriend would I be if I missed your parents' anniversary party?"

"How did you—never mind. It's your job to know these things."

Jake stepped closer, making it almost impossible for Sophia to keep her focus on the milk swirling in the small pan. "This is *not* part of my job."

You're not hoping that he'll, I don't know, have some crazy explanation and that you guys can pick up where you left off—

Maybe Theresa was right not to pass on the message that Jake had called, Sophia thought, suddenly worried she might end up doing exactly what her cousin feared. That she'd be willing to believe anything Jake said as long as it meant picking up where they left off. Did he know, she wondered in pained embarrassment, how close she'd been to falling into bed with him? That if he'd pressed just a little, she would have gladly given in? And did he think even now it might be that easy again? That she would be that easy...

"What about the mugger?"

"What?"

"The would-be purse snatcher and your timely rescue. Was that part of the job? Did you hire him the same way someone hired you?"

"No! No, I did not hire that guy!" He swore beneath his breath. "I would *never* do anything to purposely hurt you or anyone."

He'd purposely lied, purposely fooled her into coming far too close to falling for him, and if Jake didn't know how much that had hurt, Sophia wasn't about to tell him. Her thoughts were still spinning, and her mind didn't know how to reconcile the man she thought she knew in St. Louis with the man she didn't know at all standing in her mother's kitchen. Unfortunately, judging by the awareness buzzing along her skin like an electrical current, her body didn't care. Whenever, wherever, *whoever* Jake Cameron was, she wanted him.

Crossing her arms over her stomach, she pointed out, "I wasn't hurt."

"You were scared," Jake said. "I wouldn't have put you through that," he vowed, his handsome face showing only sincerity and honesty.

She longed to believe him, to trust in every word he said. Which only proved she was an even bigger fool than Jake thought. "So it was only a coincidence then?" she mocked. "You showing up right when I most needed a hero?"

After the way Todd treated her—lying, cheating, turning his back when she needed him most—Sophia had longed to believe nice guys still existed in the world. And Jake had so perfectly fit the bill.

From the moment they met, she'd seen something in Jake. Something in the golden flecks in his eyes, the faint wrinkles at the corners, the crooked smile that showed a flash of straight, white teeth. Or maybe it had been the hint of his aftershave, a woodsy scent that reminded her of home—of comfort and safety—and she'd been so sure Jake Cameron was a man she could trust.

"I'm no hero, but I'm not a total jerk, either. It may not make any difference, but I care about you. If you don't believe anything else, I need you to believe that."

If he was acting, Jake deserved an Oscar, but Sophia was no longer willing to take anything at face value. "How am I supposed to believe anything you say after the lies you told?"

"I told you the truth before I left."

Another thing that left her as confused and un-certain as everything that had gone on before… "Why *did* you tell me the truth? Why not just say you had to go out of town and leave it at that? It wouldn't be the first time a guy stopped calling."

"I didn't want to lie to you."

Tossing up her hands in exasperation, Sophia had to battle to keep from yelling, well aware of her parents sleeping down the hall. "You'd been lying to me all along!"

"That was the job. Once it was over and I had the information I needed, it was personal." His gaze skimmed over her—from the top of her tousled head to the too-thin pink T-shirt and drawstring pajama bottoms she wore to her bare feet—striking sparks that reminded Sophia of just how personal things had *almost* been. "And I didn't want to lie."

His words wove a twisted kind of guy logic no woman could possibly comprehend, and Sophia didn't even try to figure it out; she was far too busy trying to understand why an explanation that made no sense could still start to melt the defenses around her heart.

Sophia woke the next morning to the familiar sound of her cell phone. Eyes still closed, she reached toward the bedside table where she normally plugged the phone into its charger overnight. Her hand waved in thin air—no phone, no nightstand. Her eyes flew open and she remembered. Home, her parents, her brothers…Jake.

She groaned, tempted to pull the covers over her head and pretend the whole world away. But as Theresa's ringtone continued to play, Sophia knew she might as well face the music. Rolling over to the nightstand on the opposite side of the bed, she pulled the phone from her purse and brought it back beneath the covers with her.

She barely managed a muffled hello before Theresa said, "You were supposed to call."

"I know, Theresa, and I'm sorry. I am. It's just that I got home and…"

Was Jake Cameron really here, in her childhood home, pretending to be her boyfriend? It seemed like so unreal that Sophia was afraid to say the words out loud in case it all turned out to be a dream. And, she admitted, even more afraid it *wasn't* a dream…

"Let me guess," her cousin filled in when Sophia trailed off in silence, "does Jake Cameron have anything to do with leaving you speechless?"

"How did—"

"Do you honestly think after the way my mother flaunted the fact that she'd met Jake before your parents that your mother wouldn't call her to say he's staying with them? With you? That your *boyfriend* is staying with you? Sophia—"

Struggling to push aside the blankets with one hand, she said, "I can explain, Theresa." And she could…only the explanation that still sounded crazy in her own head would likely sound even more so to her cousin. "He arrived before I did, and of course, my parents welcomed him with open arms. They had no reason not to, thanks to me," she tacked on quickly before Theresa could. "Jake played along because he didn't want to say anything before I had a chance to talk to them."

"So how did they take it?" her cousin asked, her voice filled with sympathy.

Sophia bit her lip before admitting, "We're, um, kind of postponing that part of the truth until after the party."

Anticipating her cousin's reaction, Sophia held

the phone well away from her ear. Even so, she heard Theresa's response loud and clear. "What do you mean postponing? And who is *we?*"

"You don't understand, Theresa. For the first time in years, my family is looking at me without a boatload of concern and worry in their eyes. Like they're seeing me as Sophia instead of as their little *Fifi.*"

Theresa's mispronunciation of *Sophia* when they were both toddlers had been the start of the nickname that had followed Sophia well into her teens. She'd convinced most of her family, Sam excluded, to call her by her given name, but she couldn't help feeling she'd done little to change how they thought of her.

"The party's next weekend," she added, "and I'll come clean then. What's the harm in waiting?"

Theresa's silence rang with disapproval. "What's the harm?" she asked finally. "I'd say Jake Cameron is."

After reassuring Theresa that she would not be foolish enough to fall for Jake's lies a second

time—and making herself the same promise—
Sophia slipped out of bed and pulled on the robe
Theresa had given her last Christmas. Sophia
could hardly miss the irony of the words scroll-
ing across the comfortable flannel.

You've gotta kiss a lot of frogs...

She couldn't say *two* was a lot, but it was two
too many as far as she was concerned.

Cracking open the bedroom door, she listened
to the silence for several seconds before rushing
into the bathroom across the hall. For a woman
who'd only moments ago sworn Jake Cameron
was totally harmless, why was her pulse pounding like she'd made a narrow escape?

"I'm just not ready to face him yet this morning," she murmured as she pulled her toothbrush
from her small makeup bag on the vanity. Morning sickness threatened, and catching sight of her
bleary eyes and sleep-rumpled hair, she groaned.
"Definitely not ready."

Following a long, reviving shower, Sophia
wrapped a towel turban-style around her wet
hair, tightened the belt on her robe and prepared

to dash back to her bedroom. It seemed silly now, but one of her big dreams in leaving home had been to finally have a bathroom of her own—no brothers or roommates to share with. Yet like so many of her goals, Sophia had failed to meet that one, too.

Sophia took a deep breath and opened the door. *Soon,* she thought. Soon she'd be back in Chicago, looking for an entire apartment for her and her baby. She had a new job lined up, too, working with a friend who was about to start her own catering company. She would still be working in the service industry, waiting hand and foot on the rich and impossible, but it was a good job. Plus, along with handling the bookkeeping, Christine's mother had agreed to babysit for Sophia. And while a catering service might have not be Sophia's dream, it was Christine's, and helping her friend achieve that dream would be good enough. She'd have her apartment, she'd have her job, and she'd have her little one.

"Nice robe." The voice at her back froze Sophia in her tracks when really she should have started running down the hall. "And I thought the pig apron was bad."

She heard the smile in Jake's voice, but she refused to turn and face him. Still, she could feel him step closer, could sense the head-to-toe path his golden gaze traveled along her body. Despite the hot shower only moments earlier, goose bumps rose on her arms, and she fought against a shiver tracing fingers down her spine. "I—I like this robe." Glancing down at the pink material emblazoned with a crown-wearing amphibian, she added, "I think it's appropriate."

"Kissed a lot of frogs lately, princess?"

At his faint mockery, Sophia turned to face Jake. His hair was still damp from his own shower, and she caught a hint of the soap her mother had been buying for years, a clean, simple scent that smelled so much more intriguing on him. He'd shaved away the shadow of beard from last night, and she had the crazy thought that she should have let him kiss her, should have had the chance to feel the rasp of stubble against her skin…

"It's a reminder," she insisted, tightening her grip on the robe's neckline as if that might help keep her heated thoughts under wraps, "not to kiss any more."

"Given up finding Prince Charming?"

"Given up on believing in him," she muttered.

"Sophia—"

Whatever Jake might have said was lost as her mother's familiar call rang out from the kitchen. "Sophia, sweetie, breakfast is almost ready!"

Jake glanced over his shoulder with an almost bemused smile. "Breakfast," he echoed.

"I heard. Blueberry waffles with real maple syrup."

"Is that what your mother usually makes?"

"Nope. Just my favorite." And Sophia had little doubt it was what her mother had made for her first morning back.

Jake seemed to realize that, too. "You've got a great family."

"I know." She loved them all and knew they loved her—even Nick, who'd be the last to admit it. They loved her despite all her mistakes, but

Sophia wanted more than that. She wanted to be the daughter, sister, *mother* her family could be proud of. She wanted to erase the *no matter what* that always seemed to hang over her family's *I love yous.*

Jake stepped closer, regaining her complete attention, as he brushed her damp bangs off her forehead. "When you tell them about the baby, they're going to support you."

Another case of loving her and worse, loving her child, *despite* her mistakes. "I know they will," she whispered, "no matter what."

"Sophia." Sympathy and understanding shone in his golden gaze, the same combination that had so easily slipped through her defenses. What was it about Jake that made her feel like she could tell him anything? Even now that she knew better, why did she still want to open her heart and share her dreams with him? Dreams she'd never told her family, too afraid she'd see nothing but the mistakes of the past and doubts written in their eyes…

"Your family will be right here to help take care of the baby."

Right here in Clearville... The idea of staying in her hometown was so far from the plan Sophia had for herself and her child, she blinked in surprise. "It'll be a little hard for them to help when they're here and I'm back in Chicago."

A heartbeat of silence pulsed between them before Jake demanded, "Chicago? What are you talking about?"

"Chicago. Where I live," she pointed out, seeing but not understanding the dark scowl that crossed his face at her words. "We met in St. Louis, but you *know* I live in Chicago."

"I know you *lived* there. When you came back here—"

"For my parents' anniversary, for a visit." A long overdue visit, guilt reminded her, stabbing at her conscience. "After my parents' party—" and after she came clean about everything "—I'm going back."

"To raise your baby alone?"

His voice had risen, and Sophia instinctively

stepped forward and lifted a hand to his mouth. "My parents…" Her words trailed off as her worry about her family overhearing drifted away. The brush of Jake's lips against her palm sent a shiver running up her arm. Goosebumps spread across her chest, and the awareness in his gaze as it drifted lower made it nearly impossible for Sophia to find the strength to step back when all she really wanted was to wrap her arms around him, press her body to his, and kiss him until they could *both* pretend what they'd had in St. Louis was real…

Swallowing hard, she backed away on shaky limbs and clutched at the gaping lapels of the robe. "I, um, don't want them to find out like this."

It might not have been her intention, but Jake's voice was certainly lower when he told her, "I don't get it, Sophia. What's left for you in Chicago? You lost your job, your home."

She flinched at the reminder, the words harder to hear coming from him. "I know what I'm doing, Jake." She could have told him about the little apartment she had in mind, about the job with Christine and her idea of a future that kept her baby first and foremost in mind. But those plans were still up in the air. So far, she hadn't actually found that little apartment and Christine's business wasn't up and running—yet. But until she had a signed lease and business cards in hand, she was keeping her plans to herself.

And besides… "The Dunworthys offered me a great severance package, remember?"

They'd paid—and paid well—for Sophia to keep her mouth shut and to disappear.

"Money is *not* going to give your child everything he needs," Jake said flatly.

Sophia blinked, caught off guard at his use of the word "he." From the moment she discovered she was pregnant, she'd had the feeling her baby was a boy. She'd mentally tried out a dozen boy names, had pictured a little boy's room filled with trucks and trains and bright primary colors.

"Sophia, listen—"

"No, Jake." She was already reading far too much into everything little he said. "I don't expect you to understand, but I've made my decision."

Leaving Jake standing in the hall, Sophia did what she should have in the first place and hurried into her bedroom. She leaned against the closet door, wishing she could block out her own thoughts as easily.

A mother-to-be could be excused for a harmless daydream about the little boy she might soon hold in her arms. But to think Jake shared—or worse, belonged—in that imaginary world simply because of his use of a pronoun was anything but harmless.

Chapter Four

For as long as Sophia could remember, her brothers had met at Rolly's Diner on Mondays. Years ago, they'd gone there after school. Later, they'd met for lunch as long as their schedules allowed, and Sophia was pretty sure Drew and Sam would be there today.

Her hands tightened on the wheel as she came to the stop sign just before Clearville's Main Street. For a split second, she wished she'd asked Jake to come along, if only to provide a bit of a buffer between her and her brothers and a distraction from the town gossip mill. Her return was bound to stir up stories of the past, and by no means was Sophia opposed to throwing some of that attention on Jake.

But her dad had offered to show Jake around what was left of the family farm, and Sophia had begged off with the excuse that she was still tired from the trip. She probably should have been more concerned about leaving Jake alone with her father, but he'd likely be better at keeping up the charade than she. He was really good at this kind of thing. She had seen that for herself.

He'd lied to her and used her…and now she was using him to lie to her parents.

As she drove down Main Street, Sophia forced the worries from her mind as she took in the Victorian houses that lined the road—the unique color schemes in powder-blue, purple and white setting each house apart from its neighbor, the wide, welcoming porches, the turrets and ginger-bread trim. The quaint village and old-fashioned shops were a draw for the tourists and the town's main source of commerce.

Finding a parking place along the crowed side street in front of Rolly's, she squeezed in between two oversized pickups, silent advertising that the diner catered to locals rather than tourists, and climbed from her car.

Sophia took a deep breath before pulling the diner door open. If people in Clearville weren't already aware that she was back in town, they would know by the end of the afternoon rush.

As she stepped into the diner, the scent of fried foods and no-frills black coffee hitting her, she scanned the red vinyl booths laid out on the black-and-white-checkered floor and the barstools lining the stainless-steel counter.

A young waitress behind the counter caught her eye. "If you're looking for your brothers, they're sitting in one of the back tables."

"Um, thanks," Sophia murmured. She was pretty sure she'd never met the bubbly brunette before, and she'd lived in Chicago long enough to welcome the anonymity offered by a big city. She could go anywhere and do anything without a single person paying attention.

Here, even total strangers knew who she was.

Discomfited by the thought, Sophia headed toward the back of the diner, her gaze focused straight ahead. Even so, she could hear the silence that fell as she passed tables filled with the breakfast crowd and then the whispers, rising and falling like the sound of the tide.

It was all she could do not to turn tail and run like she had five years ago.

It's only for a few days, she reminded herself. *Only until the anniversary party, and then we're out of here. Back to Chicago where I can disappear in a crowd.*

Taking a deep breath, she stepped through the back archway. The "new" section of the diner had been an add-on twenty-some years ago to include tables large enough to offer more seating than the typical four-person booth. Or in this case, large enough to accommodate her three brothers.

To Sophia's surprise, Nick sat on one side of the table across from Sam and Drew. Nick had stopped joining them once he got married and

Sophia hadn't realized he'd returned since the divorce. She might have been glad to see him getting out if not for the frown on his face and the way all three stopped talking as soon as they spotted her.

You too, huh?

Ignoring the queasiness in her stomach that reminded her of morning sickness and everything she had yet to tell her family, Sophia forced a smile and claimed the last empty spot at the table. "Hey, guys. I thought I might find you here."

"Can't say we expected to see you," Sam replied, a lift to his eyebrows.

"I wanted to talk to you three about the parents' anniversary party, and it's not like we can do that at home, so here I am."

"Where's your *boyfriend?*" Nick asked.

Sophia froze as she reached for the laminated menu standing up between the salt and pepper shakers. Had Nick picked up on the tension between her and Jake? Did her oldest brother sense something wasn't quite right? Opening the menu, she sneaked a glance at Nick and immediately breathed a sigh of relief when she saw the scowl on his face. Nick was simply being his normal, antagonistic self.

"Dad's showing him around." Returning to the original subject, she said, "So, about the party, what do you have planned so far?"

Drew and Sam exchanged a look Sophia recognized all too well. "We told you," Sam said as if she hadn't been paying attention. "We want to have a party."

"But where's this party being held? Who's handling the food? Is there entertainment? Who have you invited?" The more questions she asked, hoping to spark some kind of response, the more blank her brothers' stares became.

Finally, Sam said, "We were just gonna invite a bunch of people to the house."

"What? And have Mom cook for everyone?"

"Well…"

"Sam! You can't expect the guest of honor at a *surprise* party to do all of the cooking!"

"See?" Drew interjected. "I told you that wouldn't work."

"What do you mean? It always works! When have we ever showed up at home and Mom didn't have food for us to eat?" He pointed a fork her way. "Your boyfriend dropped in unannounced, and Mom fed him, didn't she?"

"Yeah, but Jake did do most of the cooking, manning the grill."

Sam's eyes lit at Drew's reminder. "Hey, that's an idea. The guests can cook their own food and—"

"No! You can't do that! Honestly, Sam, haven't you ever been to a party that didn't involve beer in a cooler and food served on paper plates?"

His teasing grin faded slightly. "Sorry, sis, I guess it's like you've always said. We're just too small-town for your tastes."

"I never said that."

"Maybe not," Nick cut in, his first effort to join the conversation. "But actions speak louder than words, right? And you split the moment you graduated high school."

Sophia sucked in a quick breath, surprised how much her brothers' words could hurt. "That's not fair."

An argument rose up inside in defense against the anger and bitterness in her oldest brother's expression, but then she thought of Maddie, of all the little girl had lost, and the words withered and died. She couldn't know her decision to leave Clearville would inspire Carol to do the same, but it had, and no matter how many times she tried to explain her reasons to Nick, he refused to see her leaving as anything other than deserting her family—just like Carol deserted him and Maddie five years ago.

The warmth of a hand curving around the back of her neck first made Sophia jump, but she instantly relaxed, her body recognizing Jake's touch almost before her mind registered his voice. "Hey, sweetheart, sorry I'm late."

He couldn't be late since he hadn't been invited, but she turned with a smile anyway. *Playing along,* she insisted, but the awareness rushing through her warned Sophia it was more than that.

His hand on her neck flexed ever so subtly in response to whatever he saw in her face. Heat rising to her cheeks, she quickly refocused on the menu and said, "Not to worry. You're right in time."

Jake grabbed a free chair from a nearby table and wedged himself in between Sophia and Sam. Her brother frowned, forced to give up territory he'd already claimed. "Didn't know you were on the parents' anniversary planning committee, Jake."

"I'm here to help Sophia…any way I can." His words might have been directed at Sam, but there was no question that Jake had his gaze locked on her eldest brother.

"From the sound of things, we can use all the help we can get. Don't you think, Nick?" Drew said.

His attempt, Sophia knew, to smooth things over, but it would take more than that to work on Nick's sharp edges. She and Nick had rarely, if ever, seen eye to eye. Their constant discord might have been uncomfortable, but it was familiar, like the high-backed wooden chairs that had once circled Grandma Pirelli's dining room table.

Far less familiar was the comfort of Jake at her side, *on* her side.

After a tense stare-down, Nick shoved away from the table, pulled out his wallet and tossed a few bills beside his plate.

"Where are you going?" Sam demanded. "We've got a party to plan, and, dude, if anyone needs a good party—"

"Let me know what you need and when it'll be, and I'll show." Nick tossed the words over his shoulder as he walked out of the diner without a glance back.

Sam sank back in his chair with a sigh. "Well, I'm thinking Nicky should be in charge of entertainment since he's such a joy to be around lately."

Drew's brown eyes narrowed as he stared out the door where their brother had disappeared.

"Maybe we should cut Nick a little slack," he suggested with a glance at Sophia. "You coming home for the parents' party has struck a nerve."

"I'd think he'd be angry if I *didn't* show up. Instead he's ticked off that I'm here?"

Sam shrugged. "Maddie's best friend went to Disneyland over spring break, and ever since, Maddie's been dying to go. Carol wants to take her there over the summer."

"Eleven months out of the year, Nick's the one making sure Maddie eats her veggies and does her homework and brushes her teeth. The few weeks that Carol has her, life is all Christmas and Disneyland."

"And here I am," Sophia said, following Drew's explanation, "showing up for the good times..."

Running away from the bad...

She could feel the question in Jake's gaze, and the weight of guilt as Sam and Drew tried hard *not* to look at her. "Maybe I need to back out of planning anything. The party was your baby, and I shouldn't have come in acting like I have all the ideas."

Sam and Drew exchanged a look. "You *do* have all the ideas," Drew pointed out. "Don't you bail on us, too."

"Come on, Jake. Back us up on this one. We're guys, right? Tell Fifi here that we can't do this without her."

Sophia rolled her eyes, ready to tell Jake he didn't have to second anything Sam said in the name of guyhood, but before the words could form, Jake shifted toward her. He caught her right hand and ran his thumb up her palm, where he started turning the ring she wore on her middle finger around and around.

It was a subconscious habit she'd had for years, spinning the ring when she was nervous or stressed, and yet when Jake played with the silver filigree band, a completely different tension gripped her. Desire quivered low in her belly, along with a feeling of being completely exposed.

If Jake had picked up on her insignificant habit of twisting her ring, what else did he see? How easily he could turn her on with nothing more than a simple touch? How she could fall for him as quickly in Clearville as she had in St. Louis even though now—now she knew his tenderness, his sincerity, was all for show?

Stressing her given name, he said, "Sophia already knows I can't do without her."

Sam cleared his throat and said, "Yeah, well, then you know we're in pretty deep here. Especially if you won't help us, *Sophia*."

She used her brother's blatant whining as an excuse to extract her hand from Jake's. She was surprised the ring hadn't melted into goo right along with her resistance and self-control, but the silver band looked exactly the same as she reached for her purse. Pretending that she too was still cast in stone, she said, "All right. I'll help."

As she pulled out a pen and paper, she was suddenly glad her brothers had done so little with the anniversary party. It would give her something else to think about. She'd seen and even served at plenty of high society parties while working for the Dunworthys. Not that she planned to turn her parents' anniversary into a star-studded gala, but she'd learned a thing or two from Mrs. Dunworthy when it came to delegating duties and hosting an awesome event.

"Okay, Sam, why don't you and Drew handle drinks and food? We can talk to the manager here and see if they'll cater. I bet we could even hire some of their waitstaff to man a buffet table and make sure the food stays hot and the serving trays stay full.

"If we can come up with an excuse to get Mom and Dad away from the house for a few hours the morning of the party, that should be enough time to bring in the tables and chairs. Drew, maybe you can take them out to one of your construction sites," she mused. "Instead of gifts, I think we should set up a donation fund for a charity..."

Sophia's voice trailed away when she realized her brothers were staring at her in slack-jawed... something.

"What?" she asked, somewhat defensively.

"Nothing." Drew shrugged. "This is just—a new side of you."

The non-screwup side, Sophia figured was what he meant. A side she hadn't shown nearly often enough growing up. "I—I'd like this party to be special for Mom and Dad."

In an uncharacteristically sweet move, Sam reached over and tugged at the ends of her short hair, the way he used to pull at her pigtails when she was young. "You're here, Fif. That's better than a party as far as Mom and Dad are concerned, and you know it."

She did know it, just like she knew Sam was trying to make her feel better. But instead his words only added to her guilt for having been gone so long—and for knowing she wasn't going to stay.

"I can't believe Sam and Drew thought they could have a party without planning *anything!*" Sophia complained over the ringing bell as Jake held the diner door open for her.

It had to be his imagination, but as she brushed by, Jake thought he caught a hint of the strawberry cheesecake she'd ordered earlier. Sitting next to Sophia, he'd regretted his own decision to forgo dessert. Wishing he'd gone for it, too, as if that might somehow curb the craving that had come over him when she licked a syrup-coated crumb from her lower lip...

"Can you?"

Hearing the demand in her voice, Jake forced himself to focus on what Sophia was saying as she turned to face him. The morning haze had burned off enough while they were in the diner for the hint of sunlight to strike sparks of red in her short, dark hair. Her brown eyes snapped with frustration, but not even that fire could hide the panic in her expression.

"Maybe they were waiting for your input," Jake suggested.

He had his own opinion about her two brothers. While he was willing to bet neither had much party planning experience, he also suspected they were more on the ball than Sophia realized. They knew she wouldn't allow their parents' anniversary to be a total failure, and he didn't think it was a coincidence that they'd put Sophia in charge.

"If my brothers were waiting for anything, it was to stick me with doing all the work."

"They did say they'd handle the drinks and entertainment," Jake pointed out.

"Right. Leaving me to take care of the invitations, food and decorations."

"Which will be amazing, thanks to you."

She gave an inelegant snort. "I totally know Sam and Drew were buttering me up so they don't have to do any more of the work than absolutely necessary, but why are you?"

Jake definitely did not want to think too hard about buttering Sophia up, at least not if he was expected to continue any kind of conversation. Clearing his throat, he said, "I'm just telling it like it is. I mean, look at the way you've taken charge. You had a meeting with Rolly's manager and a menu including your parents' favorite foods set up before our lunch even arrived."

"That wasn't exactly hard. My brothers aren't the only ones who come here all the time. Most of the staff probably knows what my parents like to order. And with the party being outside, the decorations will be easy enough. Cut flowers on the tables and some balloons."

Her smile faded, and Jake thought about the one obligation he hadn't mentioned—inviting her parents' friends. She'd argued so strongly when her brothers decided she should make the calls, Jake hadn't expected her to agree. But when Drew pointed out she was the one with easiest access to their mother's phone directory and Sam assured her it would be a piece of cake, Sophia reluctantly gave in.

But she seemed to want to get it over with— and to get out of town—as quickly as possible.

He'd asked Sophia that morning what was in Chicago for her. She hadn't given him much of an answer, and he didn't care much for the one he'd come up with on his own. He was doing his best to ignore the nagging reminder, not wanting to look too closely, knowing he wouldn't be able to avoid the possibility if he did.

The father of her child was in Chicago.

"Jake? *Jake?*"

Realizing Sophia had been calling his name, he forced aside the memories. "Sorry. I was looking around. Driving in was my first time seeing the town. Any chance of getting a tour?"

Just as she had when Sam suggested she be the one to invite most of the town to her parents' party, Sophia looked more than willing to simply disappear. She glanced up and down the street in front of the diner like a convict on the lam. "There's not much to see."

Hoping to dispel the haunted look in her eyes, Jake caught her hand. His thumb again found the simple silver ring on her middle finger and spun it around. Sophia's breath caught, a hint of color rising to her cheeks, reminding Jake of the instant attraction between them from the moment they met. An attraction he might have used to his advantage, but not one he'd merely fabricated, no matter what Sophia thought.

His gaze dropped to her parted lips, remembering the way she'd looked straight from the shower—her short, dark hair caught up in a towel, her face fresh and free of any makeup, the clean scent of soap clinging to her damp skin.… The old saying about playing with fire rang true as his body started to burn. Breaking focus and taking a deep breath, he pointed out, "This is your hometown, but I've never been here before, remember? There's everything to see. And I can guarantee it'll all be worthwhile with you by my side, giving me an insider's view."

Sophia stared up at him, her eyes narrowing, as if mentally trying to take him apart to see how he worked without any true interest in putting him back together again. It took more willpower than he would have thought not to shift beneath her gaze. Eventually, she turned and started walking. "So you want me to show some of the local flavor?"

Again, not a phrase that should be running through his head if he wanted to keep from pulling Sophia into his arms and experiencing some serious *local flavor*.

Looking around for a quick distraction, he caught sight of the biggest building on the block.

"Is that the grocery store where your dad used to work?"

With its false front and wooden sign proclaiming Leary's Grocery & Goods, the building reached for an old-fashioned air, but failed to deliver. It was too big, too bulky, lacking the subtle charm of the rest of the town.

"Yeah," she said, her pace picking up speed. "My dad worked there practically his whole life. He started as a box boy when he was a kid and made his way up to manager. He worked for the Learys for more than forty years."

Pride or maybe amazement should have filled her voice, but instead, bitterness like black, day-old coffee dripped from her words.

As a PI, Jake hated stepping into a situation without knowing all the factors; surveillance had always been his strong suit. He could study a subject for weeks if needed, anything to find out all he could. But for all the time he'd spent observing Sophia, for all the time he'd spent with her, he was stumbling around in the dark.

"Sophia…"

"You said you wanted the tour, so you better keep up," she tossed over her shoulder as she turned a corner at the end of the block.

But that was part of the problem, Jake thought. He was already two steps behind.

He lengthened his pace, trying to catch up at least physically, and nearly crashed into Sophia's back as she came to an abrupt halt. His hands instantly rose to cup her shoulders, and for a brief moment, he felt her relax into his touch. It would be so easy to pull her back against his chest, to feel the warm curve of her body against his own…

Instead, Jake let go and turned his attention to the Victorian building in front of them. Canopied by a gingerbread-trimmed front porch, the storefront window was embossed with the words "The Hope Chest" in fancy script, and from what Jake could see, the shop sold a bit of everything.

A tangle of bracelets and necklaces spilled from a jewelry box sitting on an antique mirrored vanity. A white wrought-iron bench displayed a collection of floral pillows and patchwork quilts. Angel statues in various poses modeled a collection of hats and even a sparkling tiara or two. A partially open armoire hinted at a row of demure nightgowns and robes, and yet slipped between the off-white and pale-pink silks was a flaming-red satin number.

Jake had to smile at the sexy mixed in with all the sweet, a combination that reminded him of the woman at his side.

"This shop was one of my favorite places to come when I was a kid. Hope was always finding and bringing new things into the store—sometimes priceless antiques, sometimes a box of junk she'd bought for fifty cents at a rummage sale. Walking through the aisles was like exploring a treasure trove." She held up her hand, showing off the silver filigree band on her middle finger. "I bought this with the first paycheck I earned working here…"

Her voice trailed off, and Jake had a pretty good idea what caused the now familiar shadows creeping in. Quickly changing the topic, he said, "You know, it's funny."

"What is?"

He angled his head toward the window display. "I don't see any cartoon frogs."

Awareness colored Sophia's cheeks even as she protested, "Hope isn't the flannel and frog type."

"Too bad," Jake mused. After that morning, he'd certainly decided *he* was.

It was easier after that, strolling along Main Street and more of its Victorian houses and quaint shops. A bed and breakfast, a beauty parlor, a curio shop with its share of souvenirs....

A bell above the wooden door chimed as Sophia pushed it open and the hardwood floors creaked beneath their feet, telling stories of time gone by. Old-fashioned candy jars lined the checkout counter. Even from a few feet away, Jake thought he could pick up a hint of peppermint and cinnamon coming from the brightly colored canes.

A postcard display caught his eye, and Jake

reached for a black-and-white photo of the town taken when horse-drawn carriages still tooled down Main Street. "This is amazing. This picture was taken over a hundred years ago, but if you step outside, you can still see these buildings today."

"Can I help you, sir?" A white-haired man in his sixties leaned over the counter toward Jake, a hint of a frown pulling at his bushy brows despite the polite offer.

Jake wondered at first if maybe it was his imagination that the storekeeper had purposely ignored Sophia. One glance in her direction, though, and he saw how she'd half turned away from the man as if she could somehow avoid a direct blow from the obvious slight. Definitely not his imagination.

"Just looking," he answered.

The storekeeper's frown remained as much of a fixture, Jake thought, as the town's Victorian landmarks. As he slid the postcard back in its slot, Sophia murmured, "Nothing ever changes, that's for sure. Maybe it's living with all this history that makes it so hard for people to forget the past."

"If you want to go, we can leave right now," Jake offered, lowering his voice so only she could hear. He might not know what was going on, but he refused to keep Sophia in an uncomfortable position for a second longer than necessary. Yet neither did he want to give the shopkeeper the satisfaction of thinking he'd run Sophia out. "Or we could stay a while just to piss this guy off."

He met Sophia's brown eyes, and as their gazes held, he watched as strength and determination straightened her shoulders, shored up her spine and brought a hint of color back to her cheeks. It was crazy to think he had anything to do with her recovery. Crazier still to think he could feel a connection, a current of electricity arcing between them, and that together they balanced out each other's strengths and weaknesses....

Sophia bit her bottom lip but not before he saw her start to smile. "We can't leave yet. Not until we find you a souvenir to commemorate your time in Clearville."

His attention still on that teasing hint of a smile, Jake could think of only one memento he longed to take with him when he left Clearville, but it wasn't for sale. He was going to have to earn that one.

Refocusing on the display rack and ignoring the rush of desire quickening his pulse, he asked, "What do you recommend?"

"Well," she paused, getting into the spirit of shopping for useless souvenirs, "how about a magnet in the shape of California? A deck of cards showing off our coastline? A snow globe of the town?"

"As hard as all those are to resist, I'll have to pass. I have my eye on these…" Reaching past Sophia's head to a different display, he grabbed a funky, gold-rimmed pair of sunglasses that would have done the King proud.

"Don't even start." Sophia held up a warning finger as she backed away, but a reluctant smile tugged at her mouth.

On their first date in St. Louis, they'd taken a walk around the mall while waiting for a movie to begin. Inside a small costume jewelry store, they found a sunglasses display filled with crazy styles. They'd spent so much time trying on the outrageous frames and laughing at their silly reflections, they'd ended up missing the movie.

The film had been a comedy, he remembered, one he still hadn't gone to, knowing he wouldn't enjoy it as much or laugh nearly as hard as he had in the small shop with Sophia.

"Are you sure?" he asked, lowering the glasses toward her face. "Because these really look like you."

"No way." Sophia ducked away and insisted, "Those have 'Jake' written all over them."

She reached for the frames, but Jake didn't let go and their fingers entwined around the thin plastic. If he thought they'd experienced a connection, a current before, he had no doubt of it now. He half expected to see sparks striking where their skin met. Sophia sucked in a quick breath that somehow seemed to pull the air straight from his lungs…

The bell above the door chimed, announcing

the arrivals of new customers, and the shop-keeper called out a greeting much warmer than the welcome Jake and Sophia had received. It was enough to break the moment, and she slowly withdrew her hand.

"You know, I don't really think those are you after all."

"I'd have to agree," he said, sliding the sunglasses back in place. "What do you say we get out of here?"

"Good idea."

Sophia was quiet as they left the shop and walked around the rest of town. If the guy hadn't been thirty years his senior, Jake would have been tempted to go back to the store to make him pay for wiping away what had been Sophia's first genuine smile at him since she'd arrived.

"You want to tell me what that was about?"

"Like you said, this town never lets you forget the past."

"So what did you do? Knock over a display in there when you were five?"

"No, I lost my job at The Hope Chest for

breaking in and vandalizing the place when I was eighteen!" As soon as she blurted out the words, awareness dawned in her expression. "But you already know that, don't you?" she accused. "Bet that juicy tidbit popped up in your investigation even though Hope refused to press charges."

In fact, it had turned up during his background check, and he'd wondered if old habits had followed her to her job in Chicago. As much as he'd wanted to reject the possibility from the moment they met, the reason for her dismissal from The Hope Chest was hard to ignore. Still, he didn't want Sophia to think he was like the rest of the town, eager to hold her past over her head.

"You were young. You're not the first kid who's ever made a mistake."

He meant the words as consolation of sorts, but Sophia reacted as if he'd started throwing around accusations like stones. Her expression turned cold, and she shook her head. "No, I'm not the first. And the problem with my mistakes is that I keep repeating them," she added with a cynical laugh that was a mockery of the light-hearted sound he'd heard so many times in St. Louis.

"Sophia…" He drew out her name, waiting for her to explain. *Wanting* her to explain. Wanting her to confide in him the way she had before even though he'd completely lost the right to her trust.

He wanted it back. More than the welcoming smiles or shared laughter. More, even, than the soft, seductive promise of her lips against his, more than the feel of having her in his arms again.…

But what he wanted would have to wait.

Without another word, Sophia turned and walked away.

Chapter Five

It was foolish to have expected something else—something *more,* Sophia thought as she walked back toward the diner with a silent Jake at her side. If she were completely honest, he'd reacted better than the rest of Clearville had when the gossip ran rampant through the town.

Yet the ache in her heart told Sophia how much she'd hoped Jake would instinctively doubt what he'd found and just…trust her.

"Sophia, wait." He stopped her with a hand on her arm and turned her to face him. "Take a drive with me."

"A drive? Where?"

His golden gaze held hers in a grip far more compelling and irresistible than the one on her arm. "Does it matter?"

A few weeks ago, it wouldn't have. She would have gone anywhere, done anything if it meant spending time with him. Was it possible he wanted those days back as much as she did?

The thought shook her resolve, weakening her resistance, but Sophia wasn't about to let Jake know the hold he still had over her. Lifting her chin, she said, "Fine. But only because I'm not ready to go home yet."

Turning away before she could judge whether Jake read the truth behind her words, Sophia led the way to the rental car he'd parked at the diner.

She thought he might head through town into the rolling hills home to Clearville's farming community. Instead, he took a tree-lined path that led out of town toward the shoreline.

"How did you know about this spot?" she asked as he pulled the car to a stop at a small turn-out overlooking the beach. While the location might not have been well known to tourists, it was a frequent destination for local teens. Did Jake realize the place was Clearville's version of lovers' lane?

"I drove around a bit before I went to your parents' house."

The admission froze any thoughts of lovers in Sophia's mind. "Trying to get in some more surveillance?"

He met her sarcasm head on. "Trying to get my courage up."

The sincerity in his handsome face tempted her to believe him. Pressure built against her chest—an urge to cry combined with a desire to lash out at Jake for not being the man she'd thought he was, the man she wanted him to be. She couldn't come up with a single reason why he'd be lying to her—but she would have sworn he was telling the truth three weeks ago, and she would have been wrong then.

Needing to escape, Sophia pushed the car door open and climbed out. The sky was surprisingly clear, and she could see the distant waves relentlessly roll toward the rocky shoreline. The tang of salt and sea filled the air, but once she heard Jake shut his own door, another scent teased her senses—the aftershave he wore. She could feel him behind her, drawing her closer with a pull as powerful and elemental as the tide. She reached out and grabbed hold of the rough metal guardrail—anything to keep from simply sinking back into his arms.

The hair on the nape of her neck stood on end, but Sophia refused to turn and lose herself in the golden glow of his eyes. Eyes that saw too much, knew too much. Just like she could feel the intensity of his gaze on her back, his unasked questions bored into her, digging holes she didn't want dug, pressing buttons she didn't want pressed.

"Why did you come here, Jake?" she demanded. Maybe it wasn't fair, demanding to know his secrets when she refused to spill anymore of her own, but even if she never said another word, Jake still knew far more about her than she did about him. And that disadvantage *really* didn't seem fair.

"I told you. I wanted to apologize and to explain. I'd still like to explain."

"You were hired to find out the truth. It was a job. *I* was a job."

"Sophia."

Her hands tightened on the rail. How could the simple use of her name be so powerful, so compelling that she could feel her resolve start to weaken? She stared out at the Pacific, feeling as rudderless as a piece of driftwood tossed about by the waves.

"Look at me."

Her pulse already picking up its pace, Sophia slowly turned. Jake stood only inches away, close enough that she had to tip her head back to meet his eyes. She saw the question in his gaze, asking for a second chance, but she couldn't stop from looking closer, deeper, for a deception he might be trying to hide.

He had tried to tell her why he'd taken the job before, but at the time, she'd been far too shocked to listen. The reasons why hadn't mattered. All Sophia heard was that Jake had gotten close to her only to learn the real reason why the Dunworthys had "let her go."

The shock may have faded, but the hurt remained, leaving a sore spot Sophia wanted to protect. Her anger made a good shield; without it, she was afraid she'd be leaving herself far too open and vulnerable to anything—truth *or* lie—Jake had to say.

With his gaze still intently searching her face, Jake said, "What happened between the two of us was never part of the job. That's not how I work."

"Oh, really?" Sophia challenged.

Don't ask...don't do it...you don't want to know.

The words flashed through her mind, a warning in capital, neon letters, but she couldn't stop from asking, "So how does this kind of thing normally go?"

"Most the time, it's easy enough to get what I need."

She felt her cheeks start to burn. No doubt

she'd been easier than most, falling for undeniable charm and subtle seduction. Maybe she should take comfort that, at least this time, she'd fallen for a professional.

"A few drinks at a club or a bar or a line about being a friend of a friend, and people end up saying more than they realize, especially if you know the right questions to ask."

"But—"

He hadn't taken her to a bar or a club, and he certainly hadn't bought her any drinks. She couldn't even recall him asking any "well-informed" questions about Todd or the Dunworthys. In the end, she'd told him everything he wanted to know, but had he ever asked?

"What?" Jake questioned when Sophia cut herself off.

"Nothing." The last thing she needed was to point out how Jake *had* treated her differently and hear him once again say she was special. A few more times, and she'd helplessly start to believe it. "None of that matters anyway because you were still hired—"

"I was asked for a favor by a friend," he clarified. "Another private investigator who thought you might have information that would keep his ex-girlfriend, Emily Wilson, from marrying Todd. Connor knew the first time he met Todd that the guy was too good to be true, and he was ready to do all he could to stop the wedding. Including asking for my help."

If not for the part she'd played in the drama, Sophia would have thought the story very romantic. But it still hurt to think she and the child she carried were nothing but a dirty little secret while Emily Wilson was the kind of woman Todd was proud to show off to his friends and family.

After the way he treated her, Sophia had told herself she didn't care what he did or who he married. But that total lack of care hadn't stopped her from reading everything she found online about the wedding. It didn't help that Emily was possibly the most beautiful woman Sophia had ever seen. Todd's "socially acceptable" fiancée was a gorgeous blonde who could have been on the cover of a fashion magazine. Little wonder status-conscious Todd had thought she belonged on his arm.

But Sophia had to grudgingly give the other woman credit. In one of his messages after leaving St. Louis, Jake had told her that Emily had called off the wedding and Todd's bid to return to the family's good graces had failed. Judging by the article Sophia had read online, the Dunworthy-Wilson wedding would have been a huge event, and it couldn't have been easy for Emily to call things off only days before the ceremony, even after finding out Todd had cheated.

"So did your friend get her back?" At Jake's questioning glance, Sophia said, "Emily. Did she and Connor get back together after she called off the wedding?"

The corner of Jake's mouth kicked up in a smile. "No. He fell hard for Emily's cousin Kelsey. They ended up getting married at the wedding Kelsey originally planned for Emily."

Sophia blinked her surprised. "That's…different."

"Yeah." Jake gave a half laugh. "But the wedding meant the world to Kelsey, and well—I get the feeling Kelsey means the world to Connor."

Ignoring the ache in her heart at his words, an envy for a couple she'd never even met, Sophia said, "Sounds like he's a good guy."

"Yeah, he is." Jake stared at her, the intensity in his gaze enough to make her start to fidget and look away. "And I'm sorry you didn't have someone looking out for you the way Connor did for Emily."

Sophia had tried to keep her focus on a spot over Jake's shoulder, but at his words, her gaze flew back to his. He sounded so sincere, as if ready to volunteer to fill that position in the future. To be the man who would look out for her, the man she could count on. And that irresistible pull seemed to reach out once more, drawing Sophia to Jake, weakening her defenses enough to send panic shoring up those walls.

Forcing a cool smile, she said, "But you forget,

Jake. I'm not the injured party here. I'm the *other woman.*"

"Bull," Jake bit out. "You were as much of an innocent as Emily Wilson."

Sophia gave a short, pained laughed. "Not exactly innocent," she muttered as she ducked out, squeezing from between the railing and his immovable form.

Jake caught her before she could walk away. She should have known it wouldn't be that easy, and the frisson of awareness racing down to her fingertips and back up again would be harder to escape than his grip on her arm. "Did you know Dunworthy was seeing someone else?"

"I should have—"

"Did you know?" Jake pressed.

"No. But that makes me stupid, not innocent—"

Letting go of her arm, Jake pressed his index finger against her lips. "Sophia, stop! You're an amazing woman, and Todd's an idiot. He doesn't deserve you." Some shadow of emotion flickered across Jake's expression only to disappear before she could put a name to it. "You know that, don't you?" he pressed.

Trusting Todd had been another screwup in a long list of screwups, and Sophia couldn't help blaming herself. But after the way the Dunworthys had belittled her—*nothing more than a maid!*—for thinking she could ever be good enough for their son, Sophia longed to believe Jake. To believe Todd was the one not good enough for her or her child...

"I know," she finally agreed, her lips moving against Jake's fingers, the slightly rough texture of his skin creating a tingling friction.

His eyes darkened as he drew a fingertip along the bow of her upper lip. Her pulse picked up its pace, the awareness and attraction swirling around them like morning fog, and Sophia thought he might kiss her. She swallowed hard. Crazy to think how much she'd missed Jake Cameron's kisses—the sense of hunger, of passion, yet at the same time a tenderness and caring.

Crazy, all right, when she was now well aware

that the tenderness and care had all been a lie. For all she knew the hunger and passion had been as well.

Ducking away from his touch, she said, "But Todd didn't always act like an idiot. When he wanted, he could be charming and funny. I guess I was infatuated from the start, seeing only what I wanted to see."

She'd closed her eyes to the selfish, irresponsible side of Todd's personality, and she'd been in for a rude awakening.

"But I don't think I would have—"

"Would have what?"

"I was going to say I don't think I would have slept with him if it hadn't been for that one night."

"What happened?"

They'd changed positions with Jake now against the railing. Despite his relaxed posture, tension hummed beneath the surface. A muscle jumped along his jaw, and the skin stretched tight across his knuckles where his hands were braced on the metal crossbar.

But he already knew the unhappy ending. What difference would it make if she told him how the whole thing started?

"It was my birthday. I'd talked to my parents and my brothers, but somehow it only made me miss them even more."

The breeze picked up, carrying the scent of the ocean along with dozens of memories, it seemed. Her parents—her mother especially—loved a party. One of the many reasons Sophia wanted their anniversary to be so special. Birthdays, like all the holidays, were events filled with food and fun and love.

"You were homesick," Jake said.

"I was," Sophia admitted, thinking back to that night. "I hadn't seen Todd in a while. He'd moved to Scottsdale a few months earlier." Scottsdale—where his perfect girlfriend from the perfect family lived. Not that Sophia had known that.

All she knew was that he'd been a lone bright spot in a dull and somewhat lonely job where she was expected to fade into the background, unnoticed and unheard. It was the Dunworthy rule for "staff," one Todd frequently broke, offering a wink or a smile when the rest of the family was around and taking time to talk to her when they weren't.

It had all been so harmless until that night...

"It was almost midnight," Sophia told Jake. "Todd was the last person I expected to walk into the kitchen, and when he did..." She shrugged. "He asked why I'd been crying, and I told him it was my birthday. He pulled a pie from the fridge. The cook had spent hours making sure every chocolate curl was just right on this masterpiece for a dinner party Mrs. Dunworthy was having the next night. Todd told me to make a wish and sliced right into it." She gave a mocking laugh. "Seduced by chocolate silk."

But Todd had offered more than pie. The promise of her birthday wish coming true shined brighter than twenty-three candles on a cake ever could as Todd kissed her. After so many years spent hiding in the shadows, disappearing inside someone she hardly recognized, Todd

Dunworthy—*Todd Dunworthy*—had noticed her. And she'd been blinded by the spotlight of his attention. For him to ignore his family's blue-blood prejudice to pursue her *had* to mean he cared…

"He said we had to keep our relationship a secret." *Just for now…until I find the right moment to tell my family,* he'd promised, staring into her eyes with such sincerity, such caring. And she'd been such a fool. "And I bought it. I even thought the talk about his *girlfriend* in Arizona was just that—talk. To keep from raising his parents' suspicions about us."

Months later, humiliation still stung inside Sophia as she recalled how wrong she'd been. How she'd foolishly thought Todd might be happy about the baby. After all, they could finally come clean and open up about their relationship. No more waiting. No more secrets. Instead Todd had been furious. His girlfriend had been anything but pretend. She was perfect…beautiful, rich, one of his *kind.*

Sophia's hand moved to her stomach as if she

could protect the baby from the echo of his harsh words and accusations. Sophia was nobody. Nothing but trouble. Out to ruin his life. Two days later, the Dunworthys let her go with a severance package intended to make sure she and her child stayed nobodies.

"I still can't believe I fell for some of the oldest lines in the book. I was so stupid."

"No, you weren't. Todd took advantage at a time when you were vulnerable."

Sophia had to give Jake credit for having the grace to at least look uncomfortable with her words. She'd rather run naked through the town than tell him she was far more vulnerable to him than she'd ever been to Todd Dunworthy.

With Todd, she should have recognized from the start the impossibility of any relationship. The maid and an heir to the Dunworthy fortune? That was something straight out of a fairy tale. But with Jake, everything had seemed so real, so full of possibility…until their relationship turned out to be more of a lie than happily-ever-after.

"Not to worry, Jake. I've learned my lesson."

About trusting the wrong man at least. About wanting the wrong man?

Different story, Sophia thought as he stepped even closer. His T-shirt molded to his torso, defining his broad shoulders, muscled chest and flat abs. Sophia swallowed, wanting nothing more than to press her body against his with the same skin-tight fit.

Jake flinched at the unspoken comparison, but a flicker of annoyance followed, warning Sophia he was getting tired of defending himself. "I know you think I'm no better than Todd, but I'm telling the truth now. When I held you, when I kissed you, that was not part of the job."

His voice lowered as he spoke, the sudden undercurrent of desire revealing a different frustration. When his gaze fell, her lips seemed to pulse with the memory of his kiss and the need for more than just a memory.

"How am I supposed to believe that," she asked, her voice softer and more pleading than she would have liked, "when everything about our relationship was based on a lie? A lie you ended up using as—as a get-out-of-jail-free card."

He scowled. "What are you talking about?"

"Face it, Jake, you only let me get close because you already had a way out. An escape clause at the ready."

And one he hadn't hesitated to use the moment he discovered she was carrying another man's child.

"I don't believe it," Sophia muttered as she climbed from Jake's rental and stared at the empty space where her car had been parked. "My car's gone."

Jake rounded the front of the car to stand at her side. "Are you sure this is where you left it?"

Sophia shot him a glance and gestured to the less-than-crowded street. "I think I'd be able to find it."

Jake stared at the empty parking space as if he expected her little red compact to suddenly appear. "You're saying someone *stole* your car?"

He looked completely baffled by the entire

idea—like a kid going to Disneyland and discovering Mickey Mouse was some guy in a costume. And Sophia couldn't help but take pity on him. "It was Sam."

"Sam? Your brother Sam? Your brother stole your car?"

"Not exactly," she sighed. "Come on. Let's go."

"Where?"

"To Sam's shop."

Still looking slightly befuddled, Jake turned back to his rental and opened the passenger door for her. Sophia reminded herself not to be touched by the gentlemanly gesture. Just like she shouldn't find his obviously puzzled expression so adorable. Or the memory of his kisses so unforgettable. Or—

Giving up, Sophia sank into the seat with a sigh.

She gave directions to Sam's garage on the edge of town. As Jake turned his rental into the small parking lot, she spotted her brother. Dressed in dark-gray coveralls, Sam looked up from beneath the hood of a late-model sedan as she climbed from the passenger's side and slammed the door.

"You took my car?"

Without looking the least bit repentant, he wiped the dipstick on the side of his grease-streaked coveralls. "Yep." Glancing at Jake over her shoulder, Sam said, "Fifi was always locking herself out of her car until I finally got her a hide-a-key."

Embarrassed by the reminder, she insisted, "I haven't locked myself out of my car in years."

"But you've still got the hide-a-key."

"Not so you can take my car whenever you please! I had a tune-up before I left Chicago to go to Theresa's," she pointed out, wanting both her brother and Jake to know she wasn't the same screwup teenager she'd once been.

"You might have had a mechanic check things out, but that mechanic wasn't me," Sam countered.

"Sam, you aren't the *only* mechanic qualified to perform simple maintenance on my car!"

"Nope. But I'm the only mechanic who's also

your brother. I'll take a look as soon as I'm finished here with Kayla's car," he said with a nod to the young woman standing in the shade against the side of the building.

Realizing the other woman had witnessed the argument between her and Sam, Sophia forced a smile. "Sorry. I didn't see you there."

Locking on the tiny, pink bundle the blonde held against her shoulder, Sophia's voice faded away. Were all babies so tiny? So *fragile?* Kayla's hand covered the baby's diapered bottom. Bird-like legs kicked out in an awkward rhythm that had already worked a pink and white sock halfway off one small foot.

Sophia's stomach tumbled in a spin cycle of panic and anticipation of the day when she would hold her own baby against her heart.

With his upper body once more swallowed by the open car hood, Sam performed a quick introduction. "Kayla, this is my sister, Sophia, and her boyfriend, Jake Cameron."

Sophia had always liked kids, had done her share of babysitting as a teenager, and was always willing to gather around baby pictures to admire red, wrinkly faces. But this was different, maybe because this was the first baby she'd seen up close since discovering she was pregnant.

The tiny, waving arms seemed to beckon to her. Before Sophia knew it, she was standing at the young woman's side, hoping for a glimpse of the baby's face.

"It's nice to meet you," Kayla said with a smile that looked a little ragged around the edges.

"Kayla moved into the Walker place on the edge of town. She inherited the farmhouse when her grandfather died," Sam said as he backed out from beneath the hood. "It's the fuel pump, all right. There are some hoses that I'd just as soon replace while I'm at it, too."

As Sam went on about the various repairs, more and more color drained from Kayla's face. "I don't think I can afford all that," she whispered.

"Hey, don't worry about it," Sam said with

his trademark easygoing grin. "We'll work something out."

As much as Sophia loved her brother, she'd be the first to admit Sam's talents lay far more with engines than with emotions. But he truly was one of the good guys, willing to help a young mother in need.

Instinctively, Sophia's hand moved to her stomach.

She didn't know anyone like Sam in Chicago.

Sophia didn't need to look at Jake to know what he was thinking. But she did it anyway. He was leaning against the door to his rental car, arms folded over his chest, looking so sexy, so strong, so certain. That he was right, and once again, she was wrong. But despite his investigation, he didn't know *everything*.

"I can get the work done today, but it'll take a few hours. Let me see if I can get one of the other mechanics to take you home."

"Oh, I can give you ride," Sophia offered. She still hadn't had the chance to see the baby's face, cradled like she was against her mother's shoulder, but Sophia had carefully noted the way Kayla cupped one hand beneath the baby's bottom while patting her back with the other. How she rocked the baby from side to side in a gentle swaying motion. How she made a quiet shushing sound when the baby gave a soft, pro-testing cry.

It was all supposed to come naturally, but noth-ing from the past few years had been easy for Sophia, and this was too important to leave to chance and hope her maternal instincts would kick in as soon as the baby was born.

She could use all the help she could get and wondered if she could possibly learn everything in a single afternoon.

"Sorry, sis. I'd already put your car up on the lift before Kayla came in. I was in the middle of rotating the tires."

Later Sophia would worry about her instant reaction, but at that moment, she turned to Jake without a second thought. As if he really was her boyfriend—someone she trusted, someone she could count on when she needed him.

And having already anticipated what she was going to ask, Jake had pushed away from the car. Keys in hand, he said, "We can take my car."

"I really appreciate this," Kayla said.

"It's no problem. We're glad to help."

"I'll need the baby seat from my car, though."

"Oh, right." Embarrassment heated Sophia's face. Lesson number one—don't forget the car seat. "I'll get it."

Five minutes later, Sophia was still struggling with the car seat. Sweat beaded along her hairline as frustration and panic started creeping in. She'd pulled the seat from the back of Kayla's car easily enough, but getting it situated in Jake's rental was another story. She'd tried securing the middle seatbelt every way she could think of, but the car seat didn't seem sturdy enough to withstand a sharp turn, let alone offer the protection it was designed to provide.

"I'm sorry," Kayla repeated. "The seat was, um, a donation from the hospital and one of the orderlies secured it for me."

"It's okay," Sophia insisted, even though that

was far from how she was feeling. If she couldn't do something *this* simple—

A warm hand curved over her shoulder. Her first thought was that it was Sam, but her body knew better. Hot and cold chills radiated out from his touch, and Sophia looked over her shoulder to meet Jake's knowing gaze.

"Here, let me."

He filled the open doorway, and Sophia wondered if maybe he did know everything after all. She wanted to insist she could figure this out on her own, but the baby—Annabel—was starting to fuss. The longer it took to get them home, the longer it would be before Annabel was fed and put down for her nap.

"All right." Sophia reluctantly eased around to the other side of the car seat and watched Jake work.

His hands had fascinated her from the first time they met. He'd scraped his hands when he made a diving tackle to stop the man who'd stolen her purse, and Sophia had taken him back to Theresa's apartment to bandage the cuts.

His palms were rough with calluses, his knuckles rock hard beneath tanned skin, and his fingers straight and long. Despite the obvious signs of strength, all Sophia had been able to think of was the gentle touch on her arm when he asked if she was all right.

Watching him now, she grudgingly admired the competence and confidence as he wrestled the car seat into place and secured the belt with a decisively snap. "There you go."

"But I already tried that," Sophia's words cut off as she reached out and attempted to jiggle the car seat that was now locked in place. "How did you—"

Jake turned away before she had a chance to finish her question. Annabel had moved beyond fussing to a full-lunged protest, but instead of scrambling out of the back seat and giving the young mother and crying baby wide berth, Jake held out his hands. Sophia couldn't see Kayla's expression as she handed over her daughter, but she got her first glimpse of Annabel's adorable face.

Big brown eyes gazed out above chubby, tear-streaked cheeks. Her bottom lip trembled, and Sophia cringed, anticipating an ear-piercing wail. But the second Jake cradled the baby in his big hands—his confident, capable, caring hands—Annabel stopped crying. The trembling ceased, and her bow-shaped lips curved into an adorable, toothless smile.

"Hey, sweetheart," Jake murmured as he laid the baby in the car seat and easily buckled her in, "wanna go for a drive?"

It was the same question he'd asked of Sophia earlier that morning. As Annabel blinked up at Jake, her chocolate-dark eyes seemed to melt at the sound of his voice. And when he brushed a kiss against a small waving fist, Sophia felt her will to resist Jake Cameron do the same.

Chapter Six

The Walker farmhouse had seen better days—mismatched shingles showed where the roof had been repaired, paint peeled off the siding in differing layers to reveal the various colors the house had been over the years, the front porch sagged in the center in front of a door that—

"Sticks," Kayla explained as she turned the handle and kicked the lower right corner to pop the door free.

As Sophia followed the other woman inside, though, she barely paid attention to her surroundings, her gaze locked on the baby in her arms. She'd offered to help Kayla by carrying Annabel in from the car. Sophia had paid special attention to how the buckles crisscrossed the baby's chest before releasing the catch and lifting the child from the seat. Annabel slept through the entire exchange, but Sophia figured that had more to do with how tired she was than because of any ease or skill on her part.

"She is so sweet," Sophia murmured as she sat on the somewhat lumpy couch, studying the baby's every dimple and eyelash. Annabel had fair skin and light-brown hair, but Sophia had no trouble imagining an infant with her own features. Dark hair, dark eyes. She didn't really want to think about her baby looking—

"Just like her father."

Sophia blinked at Kayla. "What did you say?"

"Annabel. She looks just like her father."

The other woman reached into her purse for her wallet and flipped it open. Half a dozen photos unfolded. "See? That's Devon. Annabel has his eyes and his chin and long graceful fingers like his. He's a musician."

She passed the pictures to Sophia, but she barely spared a glance at the bleach-blond, tattooed guy in the photos once Jake leaned close. He stood behind the couch but rested his hand on her shoulder to get a better look. Her entire body felt energized by his touch, and she was surprised Annabel didn't wake from the sudden jolt. "What does he play?"

"Guitar. Maybe Annabel will get some of that talent from Devon since it's not like she'd gonna get anything else. He pretty much bailed when I found out I was pregnant." As Kayla took the photos back, she tossed her head defiantly. "We're better off without him."

Boy, did she know, Sophia thought, even though holding Annabel made it that much harder for her to understand how a man could walk away from his flesh and blood so easily. From the moment she learned she was pregnant, Sophia had vowed to do all she could to love and protect her child. She couldn't wait to hold her baby.

"I'll be happy if I never see him again."

The words were right, but Kayla's actions spoke louder than words as she took a last long look at the photos before she tucked them back into her purse. Love and heartbreak were written in her eyes.

At least that was one thing she and Kayla *didn't* have in common. Todd's betrayal had destroyed Sophia's feelings for him so completely, so thoroughly, so…*easily.* She'd been hurt by his insults and accusations, but not nearly as heartbroken as she should have been if she'd loved him—the way Kayla clearly still loved Devon.

Sophia sighed as she stroked Annabel's sandy curls. Her baby might not have been conceived in love, she admitted, swallowing the jagged lump of guilt at that realization, but her child would be raised in love. She would never let her daughter or son feel unwanted or discarded as Todd had left her feeling.

Sophia didn't want to overload the new mother with questions, but it wasn't hard to keep the conversation focused on Annabel as Sophia tried to learn all she could. How did Kayla know how much to feed Annabel? When to put her down for a nap? How to tell a tired cry from a hungry cry from a something's-really-wrong cry?

Sophia sensed the young woman was still somewhat overwhelmed by the mysteries of being a good mother herself and when she'd asked Kayla how she was handling it all? The girl's answer had done nothing to put Sophia at ease.

"I'm just lucky to live in a small town like Clearville. Moving back here has been the best thing to happen since Devon left. I really think my grandfather was giving me one last gift by leaving me this farm. I know it doesn't look like much—" Kayla shook her head wryly as she gestured to the living room with its worn hardwood floors, mismatched furniture and bare walls. "Heck, when I first saw the place, I nearly broke down, but it's come a long way already.

"I don't know what I'd do without people like your family. I mean, you heard Sam earlier. Who else would do all that work on my car without expecting payment up front? When I first gave birth to Annabel, your mother brought over enough frozen casseroles to last until she's in kindergarten. And then Drew sent some men over to help with repairs I needed done around the farm to get it ready to sell." Kayla laughed. "Would you believe Nick even came over to set some traps to relocate some raccoons that had moved into the attic?"

Sophia could believe it—all of it. Using their time and talent to help out a new mother in need was exactly the kind of thing her family would do. She was proud of them all, and she needed to know someday they'd feel that way about her, too.

"They've all been so kind to me. You, too, for giving me a ride home. And I've been such a poor hostess. Let me get you both something to drink." Promising to return with freshly brewed iced tea, Kayla disappeared through a swinging doorway to the kitchen.

Leaving Sophia alone with the sleeping Annabel and a far too observant Jake.

He might not have said anything during

Kayla's glowing comments about the town and her family, but Sophia had felt his gaze the entire time. "You okay?"

The deep murmur of his voice seemed to reach inside her chest and tug at all the emotions tangled up inside her, urging her to let them all out. As if he might ease those worries. As if he might shoulder some of her concerns as easily as he'd lifted Annabel.

But would he? Or would Jake turn her fears against her and use them as another point in his argument to keep her in Clearville?

"You never did answer me earlier," Jake said as he and Sophia drove back toward town. The more Kayla had talked about how wonderful the Pirellis were, the more Sophia had withdrawn from the conversation to stare intently into her iced tea.

"I'm fine. I was just thinking about Kayla and how much she misses Devon."

That wasn't the answer he'd expected, and he glanced over at her profile with a frown. "The boyfriend she swore not fifteen minutes ago she never wanted to see again?" he asked. "That Devon?"

Glancing over with her eyebrows raised in question, she said, "You didn't really buy all that, did you?"

And that was his problem, he thought. He *had* bought it all. Just now with Kayla…and for three years with Mollie.

Jake didn't know how many times he heard Mollie say how glad she was that her ex-husband was out of her life, how divorcing him had been the best decision she'd made since saying "I do."

Mollie's announcement that she was getting back together with her ex had been a blow, but her decision to cut Jake out of Josh's life had left a gaping hole he didn't think he would ever fill. For three years, he'd thought of the little boy as his own son. He'd loved him like a son. But as Mollie pointed out, he *wasn't* Josh's father.

Getting back together with Roger is the right thing to do, Mollie had told him. *The right thing for me and for Josh. It's a chance for us to be a real family.*

A real family. Jake supposed he couldn't blame Mollie for excluding him from that concept. It wasn't like he had much experience, not after a childhood where his stepfather made it clear Jake wasn't his son.

And yet that was why he'd tried so hard to be a father to Josh. No way in hell was he going to follow in his stepfather's footsteps. So he'd opened his heart to the dark-haired, curly-headed boy only to have it ripped out because in three years with Mollie, he hadn't seen whatever Sophia had instantly picked up on in Kayla.

"She'd take him back in a heartbeat," Sophia was saying.

"Would *she?*" he asked.

Sophia sighed. "There are definitely still some feelings there. All those pictures she still carries around? And just hearing her say his name. I could tell how much she loves him."

Was Kayla the woman in love or was Sophia seeing in Kayla what she didn't want to admit

about herself? Was Sophia the one hoping the
father of her child would come after her so she
could take him back in a heartbeat?

The thought of Sophia back with an SOB like
Todd Dunworthy had Jake's hands strangling the
wheel. Losing Mollie had been a blow he'd never
seen coming, but with that past experience, Jake
didn't dare close his eyes to the possibility of
Sophia going back to Todd—no matter what she
said.

He could feel the curiosity in Sophia's gaze,
but he kept his own focused on the windshield
as if he was darting in and out of L.A. traffic
instead of the only car on a two-lane country
road.

"You were pretty good with that car seat…and
with Annabel."

He heard the question behind her words, and
part of him wanted to tell Sophia everything—
about Mollie, about Josh, even about his own
less than ideal childhood so she'd realize how
lucky her child would be to grow up surrounded
by a family like hers.

But his feelings of failure—as a son, as a wannabe father—clogged his throat with regret and made it impossible for Jake to tell Sophia anything close to the truth.

Instead, he shrugged and said, "Must be beginner's luck."

A tension-filled silence followed until he sensed Sophia shift away to stare out the side window. "Yeah, that must be it."

Disappointment filled her voice, and Jake wished he could believe it was only his lack of an answer that had let her down.

Standing on the Pirellis' back porch, Jake breathed in a combination of clean, crisp air and freshly brewed coffee drifting from the open kitchen window. Vanessa Pirelli was inside fixing breakfast. He'd insisted a cup of coffee was all he needed, but she'd scolded him with a frown. "Coffee is a beverage, not a breakfast. What would you like? Any favorites I could make for you?"

A long-ago memory surfaced. His mother

standing at a tiny, dingy stove in their tiny, dingy apartment making slightly burned pancakes in abstract shapes.

What do you see, Jake? she'd ask as she set a plate in front of him with a smile. *A dog? A lion? A bear?*

He'd come up with the craziest animal he could think of in response, and his mother would tease, *You must be the luckiest boy in the world to have aardvark for breakfast.*

But the weekend ritual—and Jake's boyhood luck—came to an abrupt end once his mother remarried. Cold cereal and colder conversation in a formal dining room replaced pancakes and laughter.

Being surrounded by Pirellis made comparisons to his own life inevitable, but he'd learned his lesson when it came to family. Truth was, he was much better off without ties. Ties were all too painful when cut.

But with Vanessa waiting for an answer, he couldn't tell her his idea of breakfast was an energy bar eaten in the car on the way to work, and that was just the way he liked it. He wasn't sure what he was going to say until he suddenly blurted out, "French toast."

He knew exactly where the answer came from as the combination of flavors—the vanilla and cinnamon taste of Sophia's kiss—burst to sensual life against his tongue.

After their second date spent at a local church fair, Sophia confessed a craving for something sweet. They'd found an all night diner where she'd pored over the desserts before admitting what she really wanted was on the breakfast menu.

He should have picked up on her hesitation as Sophia had explained away her choice as a sudden craving. But he hadn't thought anything about it at the time, and once Sophia let out a sigh of pleasure, he hadn't been thinking at all. When she offered him a bite, he'd ignored the fork she held out, tasting the sweet syrup and powdered sugar topping straight from her lips.

"Is that your favorite?" Vanessa had asked, snapping him back to reality.

His answer was the same as the one he'd given when Sophia asked, desire bringing a flush to her cheeks and darkening her eyes. "It is now."

He wasn't sure how he was going to sit across from her parents, making any sort of intelligent conversation, when he knew at the first bite he'd want to haul Sophia into his arms the same way he had the second they left the diner.

Maybe he was subconsciously torturing himself for lying to Sophia, he thought wryly. And it *would* be torture. To sit so close, to breathe in the scent of her skin, to taste the memory of her kiss in each bite of French toast, knowing memory could never compare with the real woman at his side…

The sudden ring of his cell phone jarred Jake out of his thoughts. The sound seemed so out of place, belonging with the traffic, smog and pressures of L.A. Problem was, so did Jake—a fact he was having a hard time remembering the longer he spent with Sophia in her small hometown.

He pulled the phone from his pocket and answered with a gruff, "Yeah?"

"Guess that answers my first question," the wry voice coming over the phone belonged to Connor McClane, and Jake forced himself to relax.

As a friend and fellow investigator, Connor would pick up and hound Jake over any problem he was having, and he'd given too much away already. "Hey, Connor. How was the honeymoon?"

He and Connor had met while working opposite sides of a nasty divorce. After the case was over, they'd met for drinks, shaking their heads at discovering *both* spouses were cheating on each other and toasting their single status— a toast Connor could no longer make after his recent marriage to Kelsey Wilson.

From the happiness in his friend's voice, Jake doubted Connor minded. "They don't call Hawaii paradise for nothing."

"Yeah, I'm sure what you saw from the hotel room was amazing."

"Hey, we had to go out a few times!"

Shifting his focus to work, Jake asked, "Did you get the emails I sent? I've completed most of the background checks on the first set of applicants, but there've been a few references I haven't tracked down yet."

Connor had been hired by his wife's family to run background checks on a new investment her uncle, Gordon Wilson, was involved in. The exclusive Scottsdale resort was aimed toward the rich, famous and reclusive. Ensuring their clients' safety and privacy would be a challenge.

Between his rush to the altar and his move to Arizona, where Kelsey and her family lived, Connor had his hands full and had asked Jake to help out with the initial applicants, running work and credit histories and verifying references. It was a job he could do anywhere as long as he had a computer and phone—including the Pirelli home.

"I saw the reports, Jake," his friend said. "That's not why I'm calling. Have you had a chance to explain things to Sophia?"

"I've explained, and I've apologized."

Picking up on his disgruntled tone, Connor laughed. "Not getting you where you want to be, huh?"

Jake knew where he *wanted* to be—wrapped in Sophia's arms, captured by her kiss. But he didn't deserve to be there. He'd already unknowingly taken advantage when she was hurting and vulnerable. Now that he knew she was pregnant and what the Dunworthys had put her through, he wondered if the best he could do for Sophia was to stay away.

"I made a mistake, man. I got too close," he confessed.

"You think that's where you screwed up?" Connor asked, half amused, half know-it-all, and 100 percent annoying.

"Losing perspective's the worst thing you can do on the job," Jake shot back.

"Yeah. Except this isn't about the job, and hasn't been since the minute you met Sophia."

Jake opened his mouth, but he didn't know what argument he thought to make when he'd already given that same explanation to Sophia.

And yet, despite what he'd told Sophia, the way he'd treated her had been the same as dozens of jobs before. He'd found the information he needed, and he left. Even now, after following her to Clearville, he was still falling back into old habits of digging up information without giving any away.

He'd hurt her with his refusal to talk about his too-brief time with Josh. If he wanted Sophia to open up—about her reasons for leaving home and her determination to stay away—he would have to do the same.

Her brothers had been right about one thing, Sophia decided as she propped her elbows on the desk in her parents' office and covered her face with her hands. She was in the best position to use her mother's floral-covered address book to invite friends and acquaintances to their parents' surprise party. But Sam had been dead wrong when he said it would be easy.

In fact, if Nick had been the one to suggest Sophia make the calls, she might have thought he'd set her up for some kind of retribution for past mistakes. But since neither Sam nor Drew was the vengeful type, she could only assume they'd had no idea how hard this would be on her.

Sophia hadn't known it herself until she'd made the first few calls to her parents' closest friends. She'd struggled through, ridiculously grateful when she'd reached voicemails and could leave the information in a message and avoid all the well-meaning comments that dropped like stones on her already bruised conscience.

Your parents are so happy to have you home.

When are you going to move back where you belong?

You can't blame your family for worrying about you—especially after...well, you know.

No, Sophia didn't blame her parents at all. Everything that happened—all the hurt, all the worry—was her fault, a point driven home again and again as she placed more calls.

Sophia rubbed at the headache gathering in her forehead like angry clouds before an approaching storm. It wasn't that she expected her family to completely stop worrying about her. It was only natural for them to be concerned, especially when she was the only one living so far away. But she wanted them to see that she could take care of herself and her baby.

She wished her friend Christine would call with news on the catering company. When they'd talked a week ago, Christine had been jazzed about the location she'd found, a small restaurant she felt would be perfect for her new business. They'd bounced a few ideas for names off each other, and some of her friend's excitement had started to rub off on Sophia. It was a good job, and who knows, maybe she'd enjoy it more than she thought she would.

Tapping the phone, she considered calling, but Christine had promised to phone with news, and Sophia knew getting the financing together and making an offer on the place would take time.

When the rumbling in her stomach told her she needed to eat, Sophia was more than ready to take a break. She'd never been much of a morning person, but she'd come to enjoy her daily ritual of coffee liberally doused with vanilla creamer. Stepping into the kitchen, she inhaled the fresh brew as if she could breathe the caffeine right into her system.

"Morning, dear," her mother said, glancing over her shoulder from the eggs she was cracking into a bowl. "I thought I heard you up and about earlier."

"I went into the study to make some calls. I hope you don't mind."

"Of course not. It's your home, too. Well…" Her mother's smile slipped a little. "You know what I mean."

She did, and her mother's friends would all be quick to clarify if Sophia couldn't figure it out on her own. "I know, Mom, and thanks."

"Coffee's fresh." Her mother dropped the eggshells into the bag for compost before washing her hands. "Help yourself."

Eyeing the pot with longing, Sophia said, "Um, thanks, but I'm cutting back."

Her mother's eyebrows rose. "Since when?"

"Well, I guess pretty much since I went to visit Theresa," she said, managing to tell the truth without telling the whole truth and nothing but the truth. "You know what a health nut she is."

"Good for you."

Yes, it was, and from now on, she was sticking with what was good for her.

Opening the refrigerator door, Sophia blinked at the shelves packed with labeled containers. "Green bean casserole. Roasted chicken. Mashed potatoes. Did I miss the memo about Christmas coming early this year?"

"No memo. It's part of a care package," her mother said as Sophia pulled out a pitcher of juice and tried not to wrinkle her nose.

Apple. Not exactly her favorite, but anything would be second best to what she really wanted.

The tempting image of Jake holding Annabel flashed through Sophia's mind. Try as she might, she couldn't get him out of her thoughts, a craving far stronger than any she'd ever had for caffeine and so much worse for her.

They might have ridden back from the Walker

farm together, but as soon as Sophia mentioned Jake's expertise with babies, an icy chasm stretched between their seats. She supposed she should be glad he hadn't dropped her off at the house and just kept driving like he had the last time she talked about babies—namely, the one she was carrying.

He might have come after her, but what really had changed since St. Louis? She certainly wasn't any less pregnant, and Jake wasn't any more willing to accept that.

The apple juice did little to help her swallow her disappointment. If she and Jake had met at a different time—

Sophia cut off the thought immediately. The only reason they *had* met was because she'd blindly fallen for Todd's charm. But she couldn't wish their relationship away without wishing her child away, and she refused to do that for anyone.

Placing the juice back in the fridge, she turned her attention back to her mother. "Kayla Walker had some car trouble yesterday. We gave her a ride home from Sam's, and she mentioned what a help it was that you'd dropped off some meals for her after Annabel was born."

"Oh, I was happy to do it. Anything to get a chance to hold that darling baby."

"She is cute, isn't she?" she said, a little wistfully. She could hardly wait until she had the chance to hold her own baby in her arms.

"She certainly is. It's hard to remember when Maddie was that little, especially when it seems she's growing up so fast. Speaking of my darling granddaughter, can you do me a favor today? I promised I'd take her shopping for a new bed set, and I have a feeling it might take hours for her to decide between ponies and princesses and all her other favorite things."

"Wouldn't surprise me, after the way you described shopping for Halloween costumes."

Vanessa rolled her eyes. "Don't remind me! Honestly, she tried on *every* costume with every accessory in the shop."

Despite the complaint, Vanessa's smile made it clear she'd enjoyed every moment spent with her granddaughter…time Sophia would be denying her parents and her own child.

Forcing the worry aside, Sophia asked, "Did you want me to go with you?"

"Actually, I need to drop off that care package you saw in the fridge, and I don't want to rush Maddie into making a decision. Would you mind making the delivery?"

Her mother paused, waiting for Sophia's answer, and the stillness was enough to make her stomach start to churn. Her mother was always in motion, the constant multitasker, rarely slowing except to make a point. Vanessa would never purposely hurt any of her children, but that didn't mean she wouldn't give a serious push or two if she thought it necessary. And Vanessa, like the rest of the family, had seen Sophia's move to Chicago as running away from her problems.

She'd thought it would be better for everyone if she left, but even that decision had its consequences. Maybe if she'd stayed and stood up for herself, maybe then her father wouldn't have tried to fight so hard for her—a battle that ended

up costing him his job as he took on the powerful Learys. And the unspoken comparisons to
Nick's wife, Carol, cut deep. Her oldest brother
still looked at her with lingering resentment,
placing her in the same "women who desert their
families" category.

Taking a deep breath and mentally preparing
for battle, Sophia asked, "Who am I delivering
to?"

"It's for Hope Daniels."

"I saw the shop was closed, but I thought she
was off on one of her treasure hunts…is she
okay?"

"She stepped wrong off a ladder and broke her
ankle, but she's fine. She's vowed to get the shop
back open even if it means hopping around on
one foot." Vanessa turned back to the glass bowl
waiting on the counter and measured out a cup
of brown sugar as if the matter was decided.

"That does sound like Hope." She'd long admired the other woman and had once seen her
as a mentor for her own dreams. Hope had given
Sophia her first real job and taught her all about

running a small retail shop. Sophia thumbed the silver band she wore, the ring Hope had insisted she purchase with her first paycheck. Hope had trusted Sophia—and Sophia had betrayed that trust.

"You know she'd love to see you," Vanessa said gently before she handed Sophia a loaf a bread and a knife. "Cut the crusts from a dozen pieces, please."

Hope had always been far more forgiving than Sophia felt she deserved. "Um, I still don't have my car back from Sam's, though." As excuses went, that one was more than lame, and her mother waved it away.

"You and Jake can take his rental car."

"Right," Sophia sighed and turned her attention to trimming the bread, saving the crusts for the croutons her mother would make later. "Where is Jake, anyway?"

Vanessa pulled a few bottles from the lazy Susan in an overhead cupboard. "He was out back making some phone calls, but then your dad roped him into helping him fix the grass trimmer."

"Did Jake say he knew anything about fixing mowers?"

"I don't think that matters," Vanessa laughed. "I'm sure your father's more interested in male bonding time than he is in getting that old thing running again."

Male bonding between Jake and her dad… Sophia set aside the knife. If Jake had been a real boyfriend, she would have been glad to hear they were spending time together. But nothing about their relationship was real.

When I held you, when I kissed you, that was not part of the job.

Okay, so maybe the physical chemistry was genuine, but she was pregnant with another man's child. In a few months, she'd have a beach ball for a belly, and not long after that would come breastfeeding, sleepless nights and all the other demands of a newborn baby. Physical attraction was not going to cut it. Not by a long shot.

"It's time for them to come back inside and clean up," her mother said. "Breakfast will be ready soon."

"I'll go tell them." Sophia stepped toward the back door, only to turn back around again as the combination of crustless bread and batter finally clicked. "Is that French toast?"

"Sure is." Vanessa smiled as she dropped the first of the pieces of bread into the egg, sugar and cinnamon mixture. "Jake says it's his favorite."

"Yeah," Sophia said faintly, trapped by rich, decadent memories of the meal they'd shared in a small St. Louis diner. "It is now."

No one would mistake Jake Cameron as a long-lost Pirelli relative, but as Sophia walked across the backyard to her dad's garage/workshop, her first thought when she saw Jake and her dad working on the DOA lawn trimmer was that he looked like he belonged.

In a black T-shirt and a pair of tattered jeans faded to white at the seams, knees and—Sophia spent way too much time noticing—rear, he was sexy enough to pose for a pinup calendar. And yet with a smudge of grease marking one cheek and a boyish grin on his face, he looked like a kid in a candy store…or maybe a hardware store.

Jake looked happy—like the guy she'd met in St. Louis. Easygoing, carefree, a man she could love instead of a man who held his secrets close while keeping people at a distance.

And her dad…he looked exactly as he did whenever her brothers had some extra time to spend with him doing *anything*. Her mother was right. The lawn trimmer was sacrificing itself for a long-honored tradition of male bonding, and her dad was in his element.

Having Jake here was supposed to make it easier to tell her family the truth about Todd, but seeing him working with Vince, Sophia was starting to realize the harder truth might be telling her family about *Jake*.

She should come clean now, Sophia decided as she walked closer to the two men. Tell the truth and tell Jake goodbye. But her steps and her resolve faltered as she drew closer as if she could put off the future by simply refusing to put one foot in front of the other.

"Hi, princess," Vince called out as he caught sight of her. "'Bout time you got outta bed."

"I've been up, Dad," she retorted, the old argument playing like a worn record, but unlike years past, Sophia could now see the teasing spark in her dad's brown eyes. "So tell me, what did that poor lawn trimmer ever do to you?"

"Hasn't been working right."

"Did you figure out what's wrong with it?"

"Yep," Jake said sagely as he wiped his hands on an old rag.

He exchanged a glance with Vince who confessed, "Nothing a new machine won't fix."

Sophia laughed. "Well, I guess I should be glad it was Sam who hijacked my car for maintenance."

"Hey, who do you think taught that boy all he knows?"

It was a claim he made of all his sons' talents, and Sophia rolled her eyes. "You, Dad."

"You know it," he said with a fatherly pride that sent another one of those pains arrowing into her gut even as he brushed a kiss against her cheek. "Great guy you've got there," he said in what he thought was a whisper even though it carried loud and clear. "Not so good with his hands, though."

As Sophia met Jake's gaze over her dad's shoulder, the kindled desire in his golden gaze brought a flush of heat to her cheeks. She certainly could have refuted her father's statement but figured her dad didn't really want to know just how talented Jake's hands truly were. "I'll keep that in mind."

"I think my masculinity just took a hit," Jake said once Vince had made his way back to the house.

"More like a whack," she said with a pointed look at the defunct trimmer. "But your ego will survive."

"It might need some serious resuscitation first."

"Yeah, right," Sophia scoffed as if she wasn't

tempted. Seriously tempted. "Two words, Jake—French toast."

His eyebrows shot toward his hairline. "You think that was ego?"

A request guaranteed to make Sophia remember the way she'd succumbed so easily to his kiss? "What would you call it?"

"Penance?"

"What?"

Jake stepped closer. "You really think I'll be able to take one single bite without thinking of your taste? Your kiss?"

Sophia swallowed hard. Hadn't she just decided that attraction wasn't enough? That more—a *lot* more—was needed before she could even come close to considering any kind of a relationship?

And yet she could see a tenderness along with the desire in his golden gaze, the combination much harder to resist. He hadn't even kissed her, hadn't even touched her, yet her lips were already tingling, her body was already trembling....

And when he finally pulled her into his arms,

Sophia swallowed a sigh of gratitude because it would have been so, so embarrassing to fall at his feet. Then he kissed her, his mouth brushing against hers, his lips teasing hers to open, tempting her to touch, to taste.

As Sophia kissed him back, she wrapped her arms around his shoulders. The heat of the summer sun and the heat of Jake's strong back warmed the soft cotton of his T-shirt inside and out, and she couldn't get close enough. When he trailed kisses across her cheek to the sensitive skin behind her ear and back again, Sophia feared she was going to end up falling after all.

Chapter Seven

Hope Daniels's Victorian house on the edge of town was very much like the woman herself—eclectic yet elegant. Traditional with a touch of whimsical. The same garden statues, wind chimes and copper whirly-gigs on display in her shop decorated her yard amid a profusion of wildflowers.

Hope once told Sophia she opened her shop because she ran out of room for her treasures at home.

Despite the welcoming stone path leading to the front porch, Sophia hesitated. Her mother had assured her Hope would love to see her, but Sophia's knees were shaking with each step.

His arms loaded down with the meals Vanessa had made, Jake slowed his long stride to match her near crawl. "You're not that same girl."

"What?"

"Whatever happened five years ago, you aren't that same girl anymore."

"What do you mean whatever happened? You *know* what happened."

"I read a report. I'm still waiting for you to tell me your side of the story."

Hadn't she longed for this? For someone other than her family to believe in her, to trust her side of the story instead of the one the Learys had told to protect their daughter, Amy?

The girl she'd thought was her best friend.

From the moment Jake offered to stay, she'd tried to pretend his presence was nothing more than a convenient distraction, a diversion to turn the focus away from her own visit home for the first time in years, and a way to delay telling her parents the truth for a little while longer.

But the kiss that morning forced Sophia to accept what she'd been afraid to admit all along. The reality was she *wanted* Jake here, and she feared the only moment she was truly delaying was the time when he would leave. "Jake—"

Her next words were lost as a sudden flurry of barking preceded Jake's startled curse. He struggled to hold on to the food containers as he tried to shake off a gray, hairless creature attached to his pant leg. "What *is* that thing?"

Sophia peered closer, taking in a pair of black eyes and white tufts of fur on its head and tail. "This must be one of Hope's dogs. She's always taking in rescues."

"Dog?" Disbelief lifted Jake's voice above the dog's menacing growl. "I've seen dogs before. That—that's some kind of rodent."

"That," a familiar voice called out, "is most certainly *not* a rodent. Bonita is a Chinese Crested and perhaps the finest watchdog I have ever owned."

Framed by the open front door, Hope Daniels sat in her wheelchair like a queen on a throne.

A few lines fanned out from her eyes and a hint of gray lightened her blond hair at the temples, but despite the cast on her ankle, Hope appeared as energetic and striking as ever.

At a high-pitched call from Hope, Bonita dropped from Jake's pant leg, hopped up the steps and jumped into her mistress's lap with a last glare and growl at Jake. "You'll have to forgive my little Bonnie here," Hope told Jake. "She has very discriminating taste. As I'm sure Sophia will tell you, I'm not nearly so picky."

When his questioning glance shot her way, Sophia murmured, "Hope has been married five times."

With an unapologetic grin, the forty-something woman held out a hand with all fingers splayed. She pushed the chair backward with her uninjured foot, disappearing into the house. "Come on in, and don't worry about the dogs."

"You mean there's more than one?" Jake asked with mock dread.

As it turned out, Hope had four—a shepherd mix Sophia remembered from four years earlier, a yellow lab puppy, a black and white 100 per-cent mutt, and five-pound Bonita, who ruled them all.

Once Hope instructed Jake to stash all the food in the refrigerator, she led the way to the parlor. As she pushed up from the wheelchair, Sophia hurried forward to lend a hand.

"It's so good to see you," the other woman announced.

Sophia blinked back tears as Hope enveloped her in a hug scented with the same cinnamon potpourri that filled her shop. Hope was kind-hearted and generous, but Sophia hadn't ex-pected this warm a welcome.

"It's good to see you, too. When I saw the store was closed..." Her voice trailed away, filled with memories—likely the last time the store had been closed.

Hope shook her head as she lowered herself onto the floral wingback chair and called Bonita to her side. "The store is fine. *I'm* fine—just clumsy," she added with a laugh and a wave at the bright-pink cast on her ankle. "But I'm much more interested in what you've been doing…and with whom."

Sophia refused to glance Jake's way. She knew her embarrassment would only encourage the other woman, but that didn't stop heat from rising in her cheeks. Keeping her attention on straightening the skirt of her sundress, she said, "Hope, this is Jake Cameron. Jake, Hope Daniels. She's the owner of The Hope Chest."

Ignoring Bonita's fierce growls and the snapping jaws inches from his fingers, Jake took Hope's hand. "Pleasure to meet you."

Hope's gray eyes sparkled behind her glasses. "I've been stuck in this house since I busted my ankle. Believe me, the pleasure's all mine."

Jake winced and pulled his arm back as Hope's little dog made contact. "And Bonita's, too, I'm sure."

"This must be a first," Sophia murmured, hiding a smile as Jake claimed a spot next to her on the sofa. "A female unwilling to surrender to your charm."

"Not to worry, Mr. Cameron," Hope interjected.

"The ones who make you work a little harder always offer the greatest reward."

"So I'm learning," Jake agreed. He stretched his arm along the back of the sofa, his fingers playing with a strand of Sophia's short hair. Goosebumps shivered across her shoulders and down her arms. The *last* thing she needed was for Jake to try harder. Just sitting beside him made every nerve ending come alive.

Turning her focus away from Jake, Sophia said, "I hope you'll feel well enough to come to the surprise party we're having for my parents' thirty-fifth anniversary."

"A surprise party! What a wonderful idea. Your parents will be thrilled. Of course, they're already so excited just to have you home."

"Well, this is a big milestone. I wasn't going to miss it."

"But…you are here for more than just the party, right?"

"No, Hope. I'm only visiting for a few weeks."

"I see." Hope smiled, but Sophia saw the disappointment draw at her expression. "It's just—we've all hoped that one day you'd come home."

Hope knew better than most why that could never happen, so Sophia simply said, "I'm sure my parents would love to see you at the party."

"I'll be there. Wheelchair-accessible or not."

"You need any help, just let me know," Jake offered.

"My hero," Hope answered with a fake swoon.

Mine, too, Sophia thought as Jake offered to build a temporary ramp out the front door so Hope could avoid the steps, allowing her access to simple activities like watering her flowers, bringing in the paper and getting the mail. He had a way of putting people at ease, of making them feel at their best when he was around.

And yes, he'd used that to his advantage in St. Louis, but she had a hard time stirring up any anger of his deception. Especially when she thought of how he'd done all he could to make this trip easier on her. Even coming here and seeing Hope hadn't been nearly as difficult with Jake by her side.

"But Sophia, you could be an absolute savior if you'd do me one small, teensy favor," Hope added, drawing Sophia back into the conversation.

"Anything," Sophia promised.

"Do you think, while you're here, you could run the store for me?"

Of all the small, teensy favors Hope could request, that was the last Sophia had expected. "Hope…"

"You have the experience," the shopkeeper reminded her.

She had the experience all right, and a résumé that included breaking and entering and vandalism, even though Hope had refused to press charges. "I don't know if that's such a good idea."

"Please, Sophia."

Hope's tone of voice didn't change, but Sophia picked up on a desperation in the older woman's plea. Few small businesses could afford to have their doors closed for long, but was The Hope Chest in real financial trouble? If that was the case, Hope would push to have the shop open as soon as possible even if it wasn't in her own best interest.

"Remember what I said, Sophia." Jake murmured the encouragement in her ear, and she turned to meet his gaze.

You aren't that same girl.

And of course, she wasn't. She'd moved away; she'd grown up; she'd changed. It was harder to remember that in Clearville, where the past seemed to overshadow her like morning fog, but this was her chance. Hope was giving her this chance, and Sophia refused to disappoint her.

"Of course I will."

"Wonderful!" Hope leaned back in her chair with a sigh of relief, startling a small yip of protest from Bonita. Picking up the small dog, Hope smiled. "Now that we have that out of the way, let's move on to something far more interesting. When's the big announcement?"

Still focused on the idea of reopening The Hope Chest, Sophia had to mentally switch gears at the excited question. Hope had always possessed an uncanny knack for knowing when Sophia had news—good or bad—bottled up inside. Had the woman somehow picked up on Sophia's pregnancy?

Swallowing the butterflies threatening to break free from her stomach, Sophia asked, "Um, what announcement?"

"About you and Jake, of course. A woman doesn't bring a man home to meet her family unless things are serious," Hope pointed out, knowingly. "So when is the wedding?"

"Wedding! Can you believe it? This is what I get for lying, isn't it? A snowball effect where we drop off a casserole and end up engaged!"

A sound resembling a snort of laughter came from the other side of the car as Jake backed down Hope's long driveway. Reaching over, Sophia smacked Jake's arm with the back of her hand. "Don't you laugh about this! Not after the way you were egging Hope on back there."

Jake shot her an innocent look. "What did I do?"

"Agreeing that fall is the perfect time of year for a wedding."

"All I said was that autumn is my favorite time of year. I didn't say anything about a wedding."

"It was implied," she ground out.

"Just like a guy coming home to meet your family *implies* a serious relationship. Hope didn't say anything that your family hasn't already considered."

Sophia slumped back in the seat. Jake was right, and the assumptions were something she should have considered long before starting this pretense. "What am I going to do?"

It was bad enough when she thought about telling her family Jake wasn't really her boyfriend; how much worse would it be if they were thinking he was her fiancé?

Jake was silent for so long, Sophia figured he'd taken her question as rhetorical instead of as an actual plea for ideas.

"When the time comes," he finally said, "blame me."

"What?"

"I'm the bad guy," he insisted, his hands tightening on the steering wheel, "and it's my fault we broke up."

"Yeah, right." Her family already liked Jake too much. Sophia closed her eyes. *She* already liked him too much. "You've played your part too well, Jake. My family thinks you're great. What am I supposed to say to make them think I'm better off without you?"

"Tell them I'm not a family man."

Unease twisted her stomach into a knot at the seriousness in Jake's voice. "Why would I tell them that?" she asked, wondering if it wasn't *Jake* telling her—warning her—he couldn't handle a relationship that included another man's child.

Todd and his family hadn't wanted anything to do with a baby that was their own flesh and blood; how could she expect so much more from Jake? But the answer he gave had nothing to do with her or her baby.

"Because it's the truth," he said flatly. "I don't know anything about being part of a family.

After my parents divorced when I was a few years old, my mother married a man who made it clear he had no intention of being a father to a child who wasn't really his son."

At his words, an image formed in Sophia's mind of a quiet, solemn-eyed boy longing for a father figure and ending up with a cold-hearted stepfather who denied his very existence.

"What about your mother?"

"She'd had a tough time since my father left, and she was willing to do whatever it took to keep my stepfather happy."

Even if it meant making her son miserable. "Jake—"

"I didn't tell you so you'd feel sorry for me," he interrupted.

"Then why did you tell me?"

Was he hoping to warn her off? To keep her from foolishly starting to believe something real might come out of their pretend relationship? Sophia only wished that had been the result. Instead, she longed to reach out to him, to heal the pain of the past....

"I want you to understand that the closeness your family shares, that's something I stopped believing in a long time ago. But it's the kind of love and caring I want for you and your baby."

Fierce determination shone from Jake's golden eyes, nearly overshadowing the loneliness of his childhood. Almost, Sophia thought, as if by protecting her and her baby, he could give her the same love and caring he still wanted but refused to go after for himself.

"Jake…" Reaching out, she placed a hand on his arm. His muscles were rock-hard with the tension radiating from his entire body.

If they went back to the house now, Sophia knew Jake well enough to realize he'd bury all those emotions even deeper. He'd smile and charm her parents the same way he'd smiled and charmed her in St. Louis. But it would all be pretend, and Sophia wanted more. So much more.

"Stop here," she instructed when he would have continued on to her parents' house. At his questioning glance, she said, "I want to show you one of my favorite places. It's where I used to go when I needed to think or to relax."

Jake pulled over to the side of the road but kept the engine running. "And you think I need to relax?"

"Actually, I was thinking you might like to talk."

Sophia waited, expecting Jake to reject her offer the same way he had when she tried asking about his expertise with baby seats…and babies. How did that experience fit in with his certainty that he wasn't a family man? Her heart sank when Jake reached for the gearshift. Whatever had happened, he wasn't about to share it with her.

But instead of putting the car back in gear, he shifted from neutral into park and pulled the keys from the ignition. When he circled the car to open her door and took Sophia's hand in his, she realized what serious danger she was in. How natural it felt to have his fingers entwined with hers and how she didn't want to let go. Ever.

"You said your parents divorced when you

were young. Did you see your father much after that?" Sophia asked when they'd walked a few minutes, with the crunch of gravel beneath their feet and the whisper of wind through the trees the only sounds.

"No. He pretty much disappeared." Jake gave a rough laugh. "It's ironic though, seeing how much my stepfather hates my job, but if it hadn't been for him, I never would have become a private investigator."

"What do you mean?"

"I don't know where the idea came from, but I got it into my head that my stepfather was somehow keeping my dad out of my life. I'd watched it happen with my mother's friends from our old neighborhood. As far as Philip was concerned, they weren't the *right* kind of people. By the time he and my mother married, she had cut off contact with all of them."

Sophia hated to think what he'd been through as a boy—losing physical contact with friends as well as the emotional connection with his mother.

"It was a stretch, since my dad hadn't been around even *before* Philip came into the picture, but I was sure he was at fault. I told myself that story for so long, it—it was real, you know. Concrete. Absolute. I just *knew* it. All I had to do was find him."

"Did you? Find him?"

"By the time I turned eighteen, I swore to myself I would. No matter what. But it didn't take me long to figure out I had no idea where or how to even start. And that's when I found Cliff."

Genuine affection filled Jake's voice, far more so than when he spoke of his stepfather or mother.

"Who was Cliff?"

"A PI I hired out of a phone book." Jake shook his head. "He was nothing like what I thought a PI should be. He looked more like an accountant—thinning brown hair, glasses, slight build. But that's what made him so good at what he did, and Cliff was one of the best. But the work takes time, and I must have bugged the hell out of him, constantly after him for updates, waiting for the break in the case that always takes less than forty-five minutes on those TV shows. Finally he got so sick of me, he gave me a job."

"And that's how you became a detective?"

"Eventually, yeah. At the time, I was only trying to do whatever I could until we found my dad."

Finality tolled in his words, and Sophia hesitated to ask, "And did you?"

Jake nodded. "He died a few years after my parents divorced. Hit-and-run accident." He stopped short and met Sophia's gaze. "My mother knew, of course. But she was married to Philip by then and thought it best not to mention it since I had a new father, after all."

It was, in a way, the ending she'd expected, but hearing the words was so much worse than Sophia anticipated.

"Jake, I am so sorry." She wondered if the words felt as inadequate as they sounded to her, but she didn't know what else to say.

"Anyway." Jake cleared his throat and shrugged

off her sympathy as if his father's death and his mother's silent betrayal had had little effect, but Sophia knew it wasn't true. "While I was helping out Cliff, one of his cases involved a little girl who'd been taken by her father during a custody battle. When he reunited his client with her daughter...seeing the two of them together, the way they were meant to be, I knew then that it was what I wanted to do."

To give other people the happy ending he'd been denied. The lump in her throat lodged even more firmly until Sophia thought it might become a permanent fixture.

"And my stepfather is to thank."

"Sounds to me like Cliff is the one you really should give the credit to," Sophia argued.

Jake and his mentor clearly had a connection anyone else would see as a surrogate father-son bond. But she wasn't surprised when Jake shook his head, denying the ties he so obviously longed for.

"I worked cheap. That was reason enough for Cliff to keep me around."

"And how long did that last?"

"I bought out the business a few years ago when he retired. He was tired of the job and ready to walk away."

"Or maybe Cliff knew *you* were ready to take over."

"If that's what he thought, I've done a bang-up job of proving him wrong."

"What are you talking about?"

"The reason—one of the reasons—I agreed to investigate you was because it was supposed to be an easy job. Just what I needed while I was recovering from getting shot."

Jake winced, hearing too late his poor word choice. "I didn't mean easy as in *easy*. I meant—" He cut himself off. The hole was getting deeper by the second and yet he couldn't seem to stop digging. "It was supposed to be the kind of job where no one got hurt."

Sophia didn't ask the question; instead, she walked silently at his side, letting him set the pace for the conversation rather than pushing ahead. It was a tactic he'd used before, and an effective one at that.

Only with Sophia, it didn't feel like a practiced technique. Her caring and concern reached out, easing the words from him without dragging him through the darker memories.

The suspicion he'd almost grown accustomed to was missing. He didn't know what had changed, but the openness in her brown eyes was like a welcome home after a long, hard trip. Jake wanted nothing more than to pull her into his arms, to lose himself in her soft smile and slender curves and forget a world outside the two of them still existed.

Jake hadn't asked where they were going, but he knew they'd arrived when the towering redwoods opened to a small meadow and a sparkling creek. Sprigs of wildflowers dotted the grass, dabs of color flicked from a master's paintbrush, and the sky overhead was a bright enough blue to hurt his eyes.

It was hard to believe that a few months ago he'd been locked in a dark, dank room without so much as a window to hint at freedom outside. Hard to believe, too, that only days ago he'd been in L.A., surrounded by traffic and crowds and noise.

Here was the kiss of sunlight through the clouds, the bubbling of water, and the lazy hum of a bumblebee. Jake took a deep breath of the same fresh air ruffling Sophia's short, dark hair and flirting with the edge of the sundress skirt tucked beneath her knees.

"Mexico was supposed to have been an easy job, too."

"The kind where no one gets hurt," she added softly.

"Yeah. Only I screwed up."

"What was the job?"

"Bring back a kid who'd been having a little too much fun south of the border during spring break." Jake grimaced. "Piece of cake, right?"

He'd assured Ryan Nording's parents it would be just that. After all, Jake knew where the kid was staying thanks to the charges he'd put on his parents' card. So it was a simple matter of crossing the border, finding the kid and dragging his underage-drinking butt home.

Only when he reached the beachside hotel, Ryan wasn't there. The kid had flashed a little too much money around the wrong people. He might as well have painted dollar signs on his back. By the time Jake reached the hotel, the kid was long gone. He'd asked around, listening more to everything *not* being said, and discovered that the *friends* Ryan had made turned on the kid the moment his parents cut him off from their gold card. "I found out he'd been kidnapped."

"Kidnapped?"

Jake nodded. "The guys holding him were amateurs. They hadn't sent any ransom demands, probably because they were still trying to work out the details of how to deliver the note and where to set the money drop." It was a clumsy operation at best, but the captors' nerves had been Jake's greatest concern. If they panicked, Ryan could end up paying with his life.

"But you found him, right?"

"I called Cliff for backup, but I found where they were keeping Ryan before he arrived."

The memory of the dark, airless hovel where Ryan had been held—where Jake had also been imprisoned—had him struggling for breath despite the wide-open space around him.

The soft touch of Sophia's palm against his cheek broke through the dark memories. "It's all right," she said, her concerned gaze searching his face. "You don't have to talk about it."

Reaching up, he took her hand and held on like a lifeline grounding him to the present. "It's okay," he insisted. "I'm *okay*. And yeah, I did find the kid but not before he tried to take matters into his own hands."

He couldn't say much about Ryan Nording's brains, but the kid had guts. "I was keeping an eye on this middle-of-nowhere shack where they were holding him while I waited for my backup. Suddenly, I heard this commotion from inside. Next thing I know, Ryan's squeezing through an open window and making a break for it. Within minutes, three guys were chasing him down, and I knew what I had to do."

The question filled Sophia's eyes, but Jake had immediately recognized at the time there was only one logical course. "I had to let them take him."

Shock widened her dark eyes, and her lips parted. "You mean—"

"I was still waiting for Cliff, but he didn't even know where Ryan was being held since my plan had been to meet up with him in town. My car was a good mile away. We were outnumbered and unarmed and didn't stand a chance if we tried to fight..."

Sophia swallowed. "So did they take Ryan again?"

Jake shook his head. "No, I saw the fear on that kid's face and I rushed in even though I *knew* better. Even though logically it was the stupidest thing I could do." He'd let emotion overrule intelligence and the results had been disastrous. But he'd been lucky. "I caught the first kidnapper by surprise and disarmed the second, but then…"

"That's when you got shot?"

Jake automatically reached for his leg, but Sophia still held his hand, her gentle touch keeping him in the present and keeping the darkest moments of the past at bay. "Yeah, that's when it happened."

"And what about Ryan? Did they take him, too?"

"No." Jake gave a rough laugh. "Crazy enough, the kid got away. Ryan made it back to town, somehow. Cliff found him and got him out of the country, then started turning over every rock he could find looking for me."

"Sounds like a lot of effort to go through just for some cheap labor," Sophia pointed out.

"I'm sure in a way Cliff felt responsible."

"Jake, stop. Stop fighting so hard. It's okay to let someone close enough to care about you."

He'd been hesitant to call his mentor for help, still feeling he had something to prove and still reluctant to count on anyone for anything. But despite the bullet in his leg and the fever burning through his body, Jake had clung to one thought. "I knew as long as I stayed alive, Cliff would find me."

"And he did, right? Everything worked out okay, thanks to you."

"*No* thanks to me is more like it. I made a stupid decision, and I'm damned lucky I didn't get us both killed."

"But Jake, for all you know, they might have killed Ryan after he tried to escape."

"Odds are, they wouldn't have." At least not until the ransom drop had been made. "The logical thing to do would be to keep him alive just like they did with me."

"You can't be sure of that. Instead of thinking of your decision in terms of right and wrong, you need to realize you made an impossible choice, and in the end, you and Ryan both survived. Call it luck, call it crazy, but you're alive. And I'm very glad you are and that you're here with me now."

The hint of vulnerability in Sophia's expression

and the simple connection of her hand in his wrapped around Jake. At first it was like a warm embrace, but soon awareness of the secluded, romantic setting and the temptation of Sophia stretched out beside him turned up the heat. He'd tried to keep his distance, but as they'd talked, he'd instinctively moved closer. Close enough for Jake to catch the scent of her skin, mingled with wild flowers and lush grass beneath them.

Her dark, shiny hair framed her face, emphasizing her wide eyes, high cheekbones and softly parted lips. The strap of her sundress was caught on the point of her shoulder, a whisper away from falling to the side and leaving the bodice held up by nothing more than a single strap and a prayer.

Her breath caught beneath his gaze, an answering desire as she murmured his name. The husky sound broke the restraints holding Jake back. He'd wanted her from the very first moment they met. Refusing to give in to that want, that need, was the hardest thing he'd ever done. He'd been operating under false pretenses then, but she knew the truth now. And when Sophia ran a hand through his hair and cupped the nape of his neck, drawing him closer, there was nothing that could keep him from taking the kiss she offered.

She tasted sweeter than the sugar-coated French toast they'd shared that morning, sitting side by side, trying to make conversation with her parents when what they—well, what *Jake*— really wanted was this—to press Sophia into the lush, green grass, and feel the curves of her body beneath his own.

Desire pounded through his veins, heightened by Sophia's soft sounds of pleasure and the almost frantic tug of her hands at the hem of his shirt. He broke away from the kiss for a much needed breath even as Sophia's palms skimmed over his naked stomach, stealing the air right out of his lungs all over again.

His gaze locked on the gravity-defying strap, but the thin slip of material was no match for him as he brushed it and the bodice of her dress aside. He cupped her breast in his hand, running his thumb over the peak, and felt her whole body rise to his touch. As he kissed her again, his hand drifted lower…and for the first time, Jake felt the slight swell to her belly.

The baby…Sophia's baby.

He'd known for weeks that Sophia was pregnant, but the reality of it sucked the breath out of him. With Mollie, he hadn't had the chance to see or feel the life growing within her, yet he'd loved Josh as strongly as if the boy had been his flesh and blood.

You aren't thinking like a real father would! How can you when you never had one of your own?

Mollie's harsh words bit as deeply in memory as they had that day in the hospital when she'd hurled the accusations. Fear of failing *again* closed in around him like the time he'd gone surfing in San Diego—he'd lost his balance, been struck by the board, and the undertow had sucked him under. His only chance of survival had been to fight against that pull, to kick and claw his way to freedom.

That same urge rose up in him now, just as it had when Mollie blamed him for Josh's accident. He couldn't take that chance, couldn't risk disappointing Sophia or hurting her child.

He made the decision in a split second, the brief hesitation long enough for Sophia to pull away from him and scramble to her feet as she righted her clothes. The flush in cheeks and the telltale reaction as she crossed her arms over her stomach hit like a sucker punch. As he slowly pushed off the ground, everything inside him screamed to reach out, to drag her back into his arms.

"Sophia, I'm sorry."

"Why? It's my fault, really. After all, it's not like we haven't already played this scene. Only this time, you can't pretend it was surprise that made you pull away, and I can't pretend you didn't warn me." Her voice trembled on the words but then found firmer footing as she echoed, "You're not a family man."

Chapter Eight

The moment Jake set foot out of the rental car in front of Hope's Victorian, he heard the high-pitched yapping heading for his heels. This time, though, he'd come prepared. He grabbed a bag of jerky-like dog treats from the seat next to him and tossed a small piece a few feet away.

The silly dog, who Jake had to admit was kind of cute in an ugly sort of way, skidded to a halt. She nosed around the treat briefly before eating it. He had to give the little beast credit. She caught on fast. The second treat, one he tossed while walking toward the house, she snatched up in midair, and by the time he reached the porch steps, her tiny, nimble steps matched his stride as he dropped the snacks along the way.

Not that Jake took his acceptance for granted. Too sudden a movement, and he knew his pant leg would be back on the little dog's radar.

"Well, well, Mr. Cameron." Hope's voice carried from beyond the front door before she rolled onto the porch. "Looks like Sophia was wrong. Bonita isn't immune to your charm either. Another female unable to resist."

After what happened the day before, Jake had never felt less charming, and he knew the one woman—the only woman—who mattered would have no trouble resisting him.

Forcing a smile at Hope, he confessed, "I don't think it's my charm so much as it's a bag of treats." He held out the bag for Hope to see and then bit back a laugh as Bonita sprang up two feet in the air, trying to reach it.

"We all have our weaknesses," Hope pointed out.

Sophia could easily be his if he hadn't already

learned his lesson the hard way. He'd tried to be a father to Josh, but he'd been the reason the little boy had gotten hurt. He refused to take that chance again with Sophia and her baby.

He could have explained the reasons why he'd pulled away like he had, could have told her what happened with Josh so she'd realize why he couldn't be the man for her. It might have eased the hurt he'd seen written across her vulnerable features.

It's better this way, Jake reminded himself. *Better to hurt a little now than a lot later.*

All he had to do was remember Josh's accident, the frantic ambulance ride to the hospital, and the agonizing hours that followed, and he knew without a doubt Sophia and her baby were better off without him.

"You seem to have a soft spot of your own where Sophia is concerned."

Hope smiled, but not before Jake caught a brief shadow quickly hidden behind the benign expression. "Sophia is a wonderful girl."

Seeing Hope and Sophia together the previous

day, Jake had his suspicions that something about the two women and the report he'd read on Sophia's past "crimes" didn't add up.

Sophia's guilt was genuine, of that Jake had no doubt, but despite whatever rebellious stage she'd gone through back then, he didn't believe she would have had any part in robbing and ransacking Hope's store.

And as for Hope, even a woman willing to forgive and forget might have second thoughts about trusting a person who'd burned her in the past. Yet the woman had all but insisted Sophia take over running the store.

"I'll be fine, Jake," Sophia had told him when he dropped her off that morning after a silent, tension-filled ride. "I've opened up for Hope plenty of times before."

Her words were true enough, but Jake doubted gazing up and down the street with wide, haunted eyes had ever been part of her regular routine. Yet she was determined to face down her fears because Hope had asked.

The rumble of Drew's truck interrupted, and

Hope made what Jake recognized as a timely escape. "I'll bring you boys out some lemonade to keep you cool while you're working." With a last look of longing at Jake, Bonita hopped up the stairs and followed her mistress inside.

"Great idea to build a ramp over the steps," Drew said to Jake by way of greeting as he climbed from the silver truck bearing the name Pirelli Construction on the side.

Sophia had suggested Jake give her brother a call. He had some minor experience with home improvement, but nothing to compare with the craftsmanship Jake had seen when Sophia pointed out one of Drew's custom-built homes.

"I was laid up myself not too long ago," Jake admitted. His leg was getting better by the day, but the memory of the helplessness, the frustration of being stuck in the hospital still played in his mind. He'd pushed himself to beat the doctor's predictions about the long length of his recovery time and to get back on his feet within days, not weeks.

Drew circled around to the back of the truck,

which was loaded with two-by-fours, sheets of plywood and a collection of power tools. Dropping the tailgate, he added, "I should have thought of it myself, but I didn't realize Hope was in a wheelchair."

"She told Sophia yesterday she didn't feel comfortable using crutches."

Her exact words had been, *If I try walking with those silly little sticks, I'll end up breaking something worse than my ankle.*

"Knowing Hope, she's already hell on wheels in that chair. I can't imagine a busted ankle will slow her down." He slanted Jake a look. "She tell you she's been married five times?"

"She might have mentioned it."

Shaking his head with a rueful smile, Drew said, "I almost hope she finds double-oh-six soon. Past few years, she's turned her romantic eye toward the rest of the town and made it her mission to try and match up every available man and woman."

Jake wondered if Sophia would feel any better

if she realized Hope hadn't singled out the two of them.

Grabbing a few two-by-fours and hoisting them on his shoulder, Drew grinned. "Bet she went after you and Sophia big time."

"Wedding plans were discussed," Jake said wryly as he reached for the nail gun.

Drew clasped Jake on the shoulder with his free hand. "Way to take one for the team, man. Sam's stopping by in a little while, and I guarantee he'll be as relieved as I am to have you share some of the heat."

"Sam? So he can rebuild car engines *and* build houses?"

"We all know enough to help each other out if we need to. You know how it is."

"Yeah, sure," Jake agreed. No way was he going to tell the other man he didn't have a clue what it was like to have family he could depend on.

During those months of waiting for information from Cliff, Jake had wondered if the PI might find even more than Jake's father. Was it possible he had half siblings out in the world?

Cliff had done his best to warn Jake not to get his hopes up. With twenty years' experience, Cliff had seen his share of people looking to reconnect—estranged family members, adopted children, biological parents.

"They're not all happy endings," he'd warned.

As it turned out, his father didn't have any other children, and in the years since learning of his father's death, Jake had concluded it was just as well. He'd already spent far too many years trying to fit in where he didn't belong.

But working side by side with Drew, Jake didn't feel like an outsider. After they unloaded the supplies, Drew talked out a design that Jake could practically see coming together piece by piece in the other man's head. But when Drew stopped for a moment to sketch out what he had in mind, he asked Jake's opinion on the details, including him with the same openness the family had shown in welcoming him into their home.

When Sam arrived a while later, he fit

seamlessly into the mix. The easy affection and friendly competition the Pirelli brothers shared was completely foreign to Jake, and yet it was something he thought he could get used to, something he wouldn't mind being a part of.

He and Connor McClane were friends, and Jake respected Cliff and appreciated all the older man had taught him, but in both cases, much of their contact revolved around work, making it easier for Jake to think of them more as professional relationships.

Stop fighting so hard. It's okay to let someone close enough to care about you.

Was that really all it would take? For him to let his guard down enough to let people inside?

"You do good work, Jake," Drew said as they finished up the ramp by gluing down a piece of indoor/outdoor carpet for added traction.

"Thanks, but the design was all your idea."

"Hey, it was a team effort all around," Sam added.

It was the second time one of the Pirellis had included Jake as part of their team. For a brief moment, he thought of what it would be like if his relationship with Sophia was real, if the wedding plans were more than simple conjecture. Drew and Sam would be his brothers-in-law, the elder Pirellis his in-laws, and Sophia…Sophia would be his wife.

An image formed in his mind, one of Sophia gazing up at him, her beautiful smile lighting her features, as she cradled a baby—their baby—in her arms. Longing pressed against his chest, making it hard to breathe, and he ruthlessly shoved the impossible dream from his mind.

He wasn't doing this again, dammit! He wasn't going to build his world around a dream of love and family and fatherhood only to have that life pulled out from underneath him once Sophia realized he didn't have what it took to be a husband or a father.

Unaware of the dark turn of Jake's thoughts, Sam suggested, "Once we finish up here, want to go get a beer?" as he coiled the extension cord for the nail gun around his forearm.

The temptation to drown the past with

something stronger than beer, someplace far, far away from Clearville, beckoned, but Jake shook his head. He'd promised Sophia he would stay until her parents' anniversary, and he refused to break that promise.

"I, um, can't. Hope's arranged for a new shipment to arrive at the store, and I wanted to be there in case Sophia needs help." He didn't know for sure what was being delivered, but he could easily see Sophia trying to move furniture around or climbing up on a ladder like Hope had to make sure everything was just right.

The two brothers exchanged a glance. "We're all glad Sophia's got you to take care of her now."

Jake frowned. Sam's words weren't so different from his own, but he hoped he hadn't sounded nearly so condescending. "Sophia can take care of herself. I just want to be there for her if she needs a hand."

He wanted to see Sophia shed the ghost of the past, and he had an idea that was exactly what Hope had in mind when she put Sophia in charge of the store.

"Right, like I said," Sam agreed.

"The point is," Drew added, "we're glad Sophia found someone like you."

"Like me?"

"Yeah, for a while Mom was thinking Sophia had a thing for the son of that rich family she's working for." Sam slammed the tailgate shut with enough force to rock the three-quarter-ton truck.

"Our little sister and a player like that Dunworthy guy?" Drew's normally easygoing features twisted into a scowl. "She wouldn't have stood a chance."

She didn't, Jake silently agreed.

"Anyway, we're all glad Mom was wrong for once and that Sophia's with you."

"Yeah. We like you, Jake," Sam added.

"Right," Drew nodded.

"But if you hurt our sister…" The brothers shared another look before simultaneously finishing, "We'll kick your ass."

"I understand. Totally."

Hell, he'd wanted to do the same when Sophia

told him she was pregnant with Todd Dunworthy's child, only his feelings hadn't been the least bit brotherly. Given the man's reputation, Jake should have known, should have guessed Sophia's secret. Instead, the news had left him feeling stunned…and jealous.

It made no sense. Logically, Jake had understood that. He could do the math; Sophia had been pregnant before the two of them ever met. There was no question of unfaithfulness, but none of that had stopped Jake from feeling like bashing the guy's too handsome face in.

Much as Sam and Drew would want to do to Jake once he left town. But if accepting the blame for their breakup took some of the pressure off Sophia, she could lay it all on him. Even though his leg still wasn't 100 percent, he'd willingly face the ass-kicking her brothers promised, although he pointed out, "Two to one odds are better than some I've faced. You sure you don't need Nick to join in, too?"

Drew scoffed. "We aren't gonna jump you at once."

"Hell, no! We'll take turns. But as for Nick…"

"He's the one you really need to worry about," Drew finished, but his frown made it plain Nick was the one Drew worried about.

Sam nodded. "Lotta anger there."

"I noticed," Jake said. With too much of it aimed at Sophia for his liking. "Sophia hasn't said anything, but it's clear Nick hasn't welcomed her back with open arms."

When Drew hesitated, Sam rolled his eyes. "It's not some big secret. Carol, Nick's wife, filed for divorce years ago. They'd had their problems, but Nick wanted to work things out."

"Instead, he came home from work one day to find out Carol had left him—and their daughter, Maddie."

"Okay, I get why that would make Nick angry at his ex-wife. Where does Sophia fit in?"

"It was a few months after Sophia took off for Chicago."

"I don't get the connection."

Sam shrugged. "Seems like maybe Carol said

some things about Sophia having the right idea about leaving this town…"

As if that was all it took to convince the woman to leave her husband and child, Jake thought, irritated that anyone could buy into that flawed logic.

"And he's still angry. About the divorce, about how rarely Carol sees Maddie, about having to raise a daughter on his own. I don't know… maybe part of that is hiding his feelings from Maddie. Maybe it's easier for him to stay civil when he talks to Maddie about her mother if he can focus his anger somewhere else."

"You mean on *someone* else," Jake corrected, anger tensing his muscles. Sam and Drew were all about defending Sophia from outside threats, but how could they ignore how hard it was for her to shoulder a guilt she had no reason to feel? "No wonder Sophia was so reluctant to come back."

"It's not like that!" Drew protested. "Sophia understands how hard the divorce was on Nick."

"Oh, yeah?" Jake challenged. "And who understands how hard all that blame has been on Sophia?"

Sophia had never been a fan of horror movies, but she'd seen enough of them to know the stereotypes. As she moved through The Hope Chest toward the front door, she felt every bit the foolish female who leaves comfort and safety to go investigate the strange noise in the darkness...despite the axe-wielding serial killer on the loose.

And while Clearville was axe murderer free, flipping the sign in the window to "Open" and turning the lock went against every self-preservation instinct Sophia had to pull the covers over her head and hide.

But she'd promised Hope, and Sophia had to admit, the store offered a familiarity she found comforting. She'd enjoyed wandering around the shop before it opened and checking out the treasure trove of merchandise. Even back when Sophia had worked there nearly every day, something new always seemed to turn up, though Hope always swore the beaded purse or silver vase or mosaic stepping stone had been in the store for "ages."

"Shopping isn't always about buying what you want," Hope insisted. "Sometimes it's about finding what you didn't know you even needed."

And nothing in her shop was unsellable. Items that sat on shelves for months were, in Hope's opinion, simply waiting for the right buyer.

It was the idea of facing some of those buyers that had Sophia's hands shaking as she opened the door.

Up and down Main Street other stores were slowly awakening—lights flickering on, doors opening, displays rolling out to entice shoppers to enter. It wouldn't take long for people to notice The Hope Chest was open again. But it was the reaction when everyone realized Hope wasn't the one manning the store that Sophia was dreading.

She didn't know how many times the bell over the door rang before her heart stopped jumping at the sound. A rush of shoppers from a bus tour helped as Sophia answered questions about the store, the town, her favorite place to eat and the best place to stay.

As she rang up sales and wrapped purchases, Sophia realized how much she'd missed working in the store. For too many years, guilt and regret had clouded her thoughts of The Hope Chest, overshadowing even the good memories. And there *were* good memories, enough to hold up Sophia's spirits and keep her from flinching whenever the bell announced another customer.

In between ringing up sales, she kept busy sweeping a feather duster over the various collectibles and wiping down the display cases. *Fight the good fight,* Hope had always teased. *The battle against dust bunnies never ends.*

If Sophia were a betting woman, she'd lay odds on the bunnies, prolific creatures that they were. And with Hope laid up, she certainly hadn't been able to keep up with any kind of cleaning, Sophia thought, ignoring a slight twinge of unease. To the average shopper, the store likely looked the same as always, but Sophia had once known the place inside and out. She couldn't help noticing a hint of wear around the edges, like antique lace starting to yellow with age.

Pushing the thought aside, she did her best to return the store to the way she remembered even if the work left *her* feeling a little ragged. It was a relief when noon rolled around, allowing her to take a break. Hope had always closed for a quick twenty minutes, and Sophia needed the time to run an errand.

Bonnie's Bakery was across the street and a few stores down, and even if she hadn't known its direction, she could have followed the delicious scent of fresh bread right to the front door.

Stepping inside, she inhaled the sweet, yeast-scented air. A glass case displayed an array of muffins, pastries and doughnuts almost too perfect to be real, yet Sophia knew from experience they tasted even better than they looked.

"Sophia, it's so good to see you!" Debbie Mattson, daughter of Bonnie and the current owner of Bonnie's Bakery, said. "I've been hoping you'd stop by. I figured it wouldn't be too long before you could no longer resist the call of my blueberry doughnuts."

Sophia groaned as Debbie lifted a lid off the raised platter of sweets, the deep breath she took of the sweet confection already testing the limits of her elastic waistband. She'd seen an ob/gyn Theresa recommended a few weeks ago, who had explained the weight gain Sophia was to expect, but she didn't think the doctor could have anticipated how irresistible Debbie's doughnuts were.

Drawing on willpower she didn't know she possessed, Sophia said, "How about some doughnut holes instead?" She wasn't above bribing customers to linger over some sweets while they considered making a purchase at The Hope Chest.

As Debbie picked out an assortment of glazed, chocolate and powdered doughnut holes, Sophia added, "I also wanted to stop by to talk to you about getting a cake for my parents' anniversary party this weekend. I'm sorry about the late notice, but we're trying to keep it a surprise."

Debbie folded the edges of the box together into a handle and set it on the counter before grabbing an album from behind the register. "I have some pictures if you want to take a look."

Sophia already had the perfect cake in mind, and Debbie didn't disappoint. As Sophia flipped through the pages, an elaborate three-tier cake adorned with deep red roses, green leaves and elegant pearls caught her eye and she knew she'd found the one. "This one. It's exactly what I want for my parents' anniversary party."

Debbie swung the book back around to face her. "I don't think I need to tell you that's a wedding cake."

"That's why it's perfect," Sophia said, anticipation starting to override her worries about the party. "My parents had a homemade wedding cake—a simple sheet cake—and I know my mother always felt she'd missed out a little by not having a 'real' wedding cake."

"What a great idea!" Debbie pulled out an

order form and starting filling out the information. "Do you know what cake flavor and filling you want, or is a taste test in order?"

Her blue eyes sparkled from her slightly plump face. Even in high school, Debbie had been perfectly happy with her full-sized figure.

"Running a bakery is in my genes," she had often quipped. *"That's why I wear a size fourteen."*

"As much as I would love to try every kind," Sophia mused, "lemon with buttercream icing is my parents' favorite."

"Mmm, one of my favorites, too. But then again, aren't they all?" Debbie sighed. "I suppose I might be more inclined to think about my weight if I had a boyfriend like yours watching my figure."

Sophia forced a smile. This was what she wanted, right? For her pretend relationship with Jake to defuse local gossip? It might have worked, too, only her feelings for Jake were all too real…

"I guess I shouldn't be surprised how quickly gossip spreads."

Debbie waved a dismissive hand. "What are you worried about? If I had a boyfriend who looked like that, I'd hand out fliers."

Her words startled a laugh out of Sophia, but she sobered as she added, "I think I'd rather lie low. I've already given people enough to talk about."

The blonde tore off the top copy of the two-part form. "You know small towns. There'll always be talk. Doesn't mean everyone believes it. In fact, most people know better, especially when it comes to anything Marlene Leary has to say. Hey, a bunch of us are getting together tomorrow night at Sullivan's Bar for Billy Cummings's birthday. You should come."

Billy had gone to school with Sophia's brothers and was still a good friend, but Sophia hesitated. "I don't know about a party…"

"Just think about it," Debbie encouraged. "You have friends here, Sophia. You always did."

The unexpected support tightened Sophia's

throat with unshed tears. She'd been so sure everyone held her solely responsible. Maybe she'd been as quick to assume the worst about the town as she'd had been to believe they assumed the worst of her.

The bell above the door rang, and Sophia quickly ducked her head, embarrassed to think of anyone finding her crying over Debbie's pastries on her first day back at The Hope Chest.

Sophia had barely registered the other woman's bright greeting when Jake's murmur reached her. "You okay?"

He stepped between Sophia and the glass case, shielding her from Debbie's view with the width of his chest. A dark frown drew his eyebrows together, and he shot a suspicious glance over his shoulder. The fierce, protective warrior was back, ready to defend her against every threat except for the one he posed to her heart.

"I'm fine. Really," she insisted when his golden eyes searched hers, concern written in his gaze. It would be so easy to believe he cared…

It's all pretend, she insisted despite a very real

shiver of awareness chasing goose bumps down her spine from the spot where Jake rested his hand against the nape of her neck and back up again.

Reality was Jake pulling away from her at the creek, unable—or *unwilling*—to accept that she was carrying another man's child. No one had to tell Sophia how big of a burden that was. Todd hadn't even been willing to step up and accept responsibility, and *he* was the father of her baby.

Did she really expect that Jake could somehow look past that? That he would want her enough that he would want her child as well?

Yes, her bruised heart whispered. It was exactly what she had foolishly hoped for, that he would want her enough that nothing, *nothing,* else would matter.

Like the way she wanted him.

Sophia knew only a little about Jake's life in L.A., yet when he kissed her, she could think of nothing beyond the moment when his lips touched hers, nothing beyond the eternity when he broke away for a quick breath to the split second when he came back to her.

Even her own past faded away until she no longer remembered the lessons Todd had taught her. Lessons in protecting her heart and not hoping for the impossible.

She should be glad Jake had stopped when he had, Sophia decided firmly. She wouldn't forget again. The next time he kissed her—

"Sophia." Desire darkened Jake's eyes, tensing the muscles in his body, and making her aware that in thinking about his kiss, her focus had arrowed in on his mouth, mere inches from her own.

Longing threatened to turn her bones to warm caramel. In another minute, she'd melt into a puddle at Jake's feet. And there was something she was supposed to remember…what had she been thinking about? Oh, yeah, the next time Jake kissed her.…

If she leaned forward just an inch, the next time Jake kissed her could be right here, right now.

"Ahem." The polite clearing of a throat wasn't

enough to prepare Sophia for Debbie's next comment, "Keep generating that kind of heat, and you two are gonna burn my buns."

Embarrassed, she jerked her gaze away from Jake's and tried to look somewhere, anywhere other than at the two people with her in the bakery. She did a quick double-take when, sure enough, a dozen or so buns were cooling on a wire rack behind the counter.

Caught between the need to hide and an absurd desire to laugh, Sophia made a quick introduction, "Jake, this is Debbie Mattson. We went to school together, and I stopped by to—"

"Look at wedding cakes," the blonde interjected with a guileless smile.

Sophia had to give Jake credit; he didn't so much as blink. "Did Sophia tell you strawberry filling is my favorite?"

But then again, Jake wasn't the one having trouble remembering all this wasn't real. He was the one who already had the reason for their breakup in mind. He wasn't a family man.

"What are you doing here, Jake?" Sophia

asked, her voice a bit sharper than she'd intended.

"When I saw the sign in the shop, I figured you couldn't go far in twenty minutes. I spotted you through the window. I'm going to stick around this afternoon for the delivery Hope scheduled."

"I told you I can handle it," Sophia protested, continuing her argument from that morning.

Jake raised his hands in an innocent gesture. "Hey, I'll be there for heavy lifting only."

"Don't argue when a man offers to do *one* of the things he's good for," Debbie advised, the suggestive lift to her eyebrows acknowledging the *other* things men were good for.

Sophia was saved from coming up with an answer by the rumble of a diesel engine. "Speaking of delivery trucks," Jake said as he glanced out the window. "Do you think—"

"Oh, great. It's the one Hope's been waiting for, I'm sure of it."

He caught Sophia's arm when she would have raced out of the store and took the keys from her hand. "Finish up here. I'll go help the guy get started."

As the two women watched from the window as Jake crossed the street in an easy jog, Debbie sighed. "Forget fliers. I'd rent a billboard."

As Sophia made her way back to the shop a few minutes later, she didn't notice the small crowd gathered on the sidewalk until she'd nearly stepped into the middle of the group. She tried to skirt around the edges and slip by unnoticed, but judging by the way all conversation stopped, she'd failed miserably.

A familiar voice, raised loud enough to carry, stopped her in her tracks. "I don't know what that woman was thinking. It will serve Hope Daniels right if Sophia Pirelli robs the store blind."

As befitted her position as one of the wealthiest women in town, Marlene Leary looked perfectly put together in an ice-blue pantsuit with matching shoes while everyone else wore jeans and boots, her blond hair expensively and expertly styled thanks to frequent trips to one of the top salons in San Francisco. But Sophia was shocked by how Marlene had aged in the past five years, as if all the life had been slowly drained from her and replaced with a corrosive bitterness.

Certainly Marlene's words ate like acid in Sophia's stomach, but the slow burn turned into cold shock when she saw the sheriff's car parked in front of Hope's shop.

Chapter Nine

Seeing the sheriff's car, Sophia broke into a run. Her thoughts raced as fast as her steps against the sidewalk. What could have happened? She'd barely been gone fifteen minutes, and she'd locked the door before she left—hadn't she?

She remembered putting the sign in the window, the hands on the plastic clock turned to twelve-twenty, and then she'd locked the door. She was sure of it! She'd even double checked by testing the handle before walking down to Bonnie's…where she'd given the keys to Jake.

She'd just reached the front of the shop when

the door opened and Jake and Sheriff Cummings stepped out, talking like old friends. Settling his hat onto his salt-and pepper hair, he advised Jake, "You need a furniture dolly to move that stuff or you're gonna be needing a wheelchair." The sheriff tipped his hat in greeting as he caught sight of her. "Sophia."

Despite his smile, Sophia could only think about the last time she'd seen him—down at the station where he'd questioned her about the break-in and damage done at Hope's shop.

"You aren't doing yourself any kind of favor by protecting your friends," he'd told her.

"They aren't my friends!" she shot back. *"None of them are my friends!"*

"I hear you were over at Bonnie's. I don't suppose you noticed if she has any Boston creams this morning, did you?" He rolled his eyes toward Jake. "I know what you're thinking, but there is nothing cliché about these doughnuts." Sophia barely managed a response before the sheriff started over to the bakery, passing by the still-gathered crowd as he went.

"Are you okay?" she asked Jake, even though she could see for herself he looked relaxed despite his run-in with the suddenly amiable sheriff.

"I was about to ask you the same thing." Sliding his hand to the small of her back, he led her into the store and onto a leopard-print settee away from the front window.

"What happened? Why was the sheriff here?"

"I met the delivery truck out front and had the driver pull around back. One of the other shopkeepers saw a strange guy and a moving van outside a store that had been closed and assumed I was up to no good."

Jake leaned back against the settee, as calm now as he'd been while talking to the sheriff, and Sophia could only stare at him. "Someone called the cops on you! Why aren't you more upset about this?"

"It's not the first time."

"What?"

"Think about my job. Part of being an investigator is to follow a suspect around. If I'm parked too long on a street filled with watchful neighbors, sometimes the cops get called. Same thing happened here."

"Watchful neighbors," she echoed. "I wish I could believe that's all it was."

"But you don't."

"I think they called the sheriff because of me. Because of what happened before I left."

"Are you ready to tell me what really happened? Because I know you'd no more rob and ransack this place than you'd burn down the church where your parents got married."

"You sound so sure, but you didn't know me then."

"I know you now. I know you love this place," he said simply. "I saw it this morning when you opened up the shop. It was obvious every time you so much as touch one of the pieces."

"I do love this shop," Sophia admitted. "I have ever since I was a little kid. Coming here felt like exploring a treasure trove of riches. I didn't care about buying things. I had so much fun simply looking."

"No wonder Hope offered you a job."

Sophia cringed. "By that time, I wasn't the best bet to win employee of the month. My brothers all were born knowing what they wanted to do. My mother has pictures of them as little kids—Nick with his dog, Scout, Drew building skyscrapers out of Legos, and Sam always surrounded by cars and trucks. While I—I tried everything."

And failed at everything...

"For a while, I tagged along after my brothers, but nothing they did interested me. I even tried all the things I thought I was supposed to like— singing lessons, dance classes, band practice. Nothing stuck. My parents were frustrated, and I can't blame them. They kept accusing me of quitting too easily, and finally I just...stopped trying at all. I dropped out of all extracurricular activities, my grades started to slide, and I had nothing but time on my hands.

"And once Amy Leary and I started hanging out more and more, it didn't take long for us to discover one thing we were really good at was getting into trouble—and getting away with it."

The worst part had been how little they cared when someone else took the blame—the stock boy who'd been fired for supplying beer from the Learys' store for one of their parties; the too-eager-to-please freshman who'd gotten caught trying to steal a test because they'd asked him to; the football players who'd been suspended for painting the opposing school's end zone with the name of their own team—an idea they had come up with.

"The Learys are one of the wealthiest families in town, and both Amy's parents have a great deal of influence. No matter what she did, Amy was untouchable, and since Amy and I were always together, that get-out-of-jail-free card extended to me, too."

Until the tables turned, and Sophia was the one to take the fall.

"I still don't know why Hope offered me the job. Maybe as a favor to my parents or maybe because that's the way she is—always trying to give a helping hand when it's needed."

And Sophia had certainly needed it as the pranks and partying started spiraling out of control. The job had pulled her away from a dangerous edge. But even as Sophia took that step back, Amy had inched even closer to crossing that line.

They'd drifted apart as Sophia started spending more and more hours at the store. And when she tried making time for her friend, she sensed a change in Amy, a bitterness and anger, that worried Sophia.

Amy had always been reckless and wild, traits that had appealed to Sophia as she struggled to find her own place in her family. But this darker side of Amy, and her refusal to talk about what was going on, drove a wedge through their friendship.

One Sophia had taken a foolish chance to try to repair.

"One day, Hope received a shipment of vintage dresses. Gorgeous, nineteen-twenty-era flapper styles. I fell in love with them all and bought one for senior prom. I thought maybe Amy would like to see them. At first, she said she wouldn't be caught dead in moldy old hand-me-downs and we got in a big fight. I thought our friendship was over after that, but the night before the dance, Amy called to apologize. She said she wanted to see the dresses after all. I told her we'd go try them on first thing in the morning."

But Amy had said that would be too late. She and her mother had planned to drive into Sacramento early the next morning to find a dress. Amy needed to see the vintage gowns that night.

"I really don't think this is a good idea," Sophia whispered as she unlocked the back door to The Hope Chest.

"Why not? You open up the store all the time," Amy pointed out, her face ghostly in the glow from the overhead security light.

"When I'm scheduled to start the morning shift, not after hours when no one's supposed to be here."

"One quick look."

Sophia thought of the dress sure to fit Amy—a white sheath with silver fringe and a row of clear blue crystals beneath the bodice. From the moment she saw the dress, Sophia knew it would be perfect with Amy's blond hair, fair skin and blue eyes.

"What will it hurt?" Amy pressed, and in that moment, in the poor light, her eyes looked just like those crystals—pale, cold and hard.

"We kept the lights off, hoping no one would notice we were inside, and when I heard the first crash, I actually thought Amy and I had interrupted an intruder. I had no idea Amy purposely tricked me into opening the store so she could let them in."

Images flickered through her mind like the waving flashlights slicing through the darkness—a hooded shadow at the register, another at a display case, and Amy, spraying the gorgeous array of dresses with angry splashes of red.

"What no one knew—" at least, Sophia had always *hoped* Amy hadn't known "—was that

Hope was having work done on her house and had spent the night in the small apartment above the store. When she heard the noise, she came down to investigate."

"That does seem like something she would do."

"One of the guys pushed her out of the way as he ran for the door. When she fell and didn't get up…" Until that moment, Sophia had felt like she was sleepwalking through a nightmare. Reality shocked her awake with a cold hard slap when she realized Hope was hurt. "I called the sheriff and waited with Hope."

"Waited to get caught."

"I couldn't leave her. I wouldn't, so yeah, even after Amy and her friends took off, I stayed. Besides, it was my fault. I deserved to get caught."

"You didn't know what Amy planned."

"I *knew* opening the store was wrong, so everything that happened after that pretty much falls on me no matter what I did or didn't know."

"Is that what the sheriff told you?" Jake asked,

seeming to have heard the echo of the other man's voice in her words.

"He had a point."

"But he didn't have the whole story."

Sophia shoved away from the settee, needing to walk off the anger and hurt she still felt after all this time. "Oh, I told him the whole story."

"He didn't believe you?"

"I think he wanted to, but he also thought I knew who the guys were, that I was trying to protect them. But I wasn't."

"And what about Amy?"

"Amy didn't need *my* protection. She had her parents."

"What do you mean?"

"According to the Learys, at the time of the break-in, they were all watching a movie together. Family night, you know."

And the more Sophia protested her innocence, the more the town's opinion turned against her. It was her word versus the Learys', and Sophia had come across as a liar who tried to blame Amy for her own mistakes.

"So they all got away with it."

"That's the one good thing. They didn't get away with much. The one guy never did get the register open, and the other dropped the bag of jewelry he'd taken from the display cases. Amy's the only one who caused any real damage."

Irreparable damage...and not limited to the vintage dresses.

"Did you ever ask her why she did it?"

Sophia sank back down beside Jake, her hands twisted together as she spun her silver ring between her thumb and middle finger. "We never talked after that night. I don't know if her parents tried keeping her away from me. Or maybe I'd served my purpose, and that was it. After graduation, she went to college in Washington. She has a job at a radio station in Seattle. Like she'd always wanted.

"The truth is, I still don't know why she would use me like that. Why go after Hope's shop? Just for kicks?" Sophia gave a sharp laugh that felt like it cut holes in her chest. "My father quit his job after that! And my mom... She used to be on dozens of these local committees, along with Marlene Leary, but that all changed. I think even my brothers' businesses suffered for a while, although they never said anything."

Reaching over, Jake took Sophia's hand, brushing his thumb against the ring on her middle finger. "Your dad, your mom, your brothers," he recounted thoughtfully. "You know, I have to say, it seems like they're doing okay now."

"I think so. But—"

"And they all seem happy," Jake added. "Well, except for Nick," he conceded. "But the others?"

"Yes, I think the rest of my family is very happy."

"So when is it your turn?"

"What?"

"When is it okay for you to forget about the past? When is it your turn to be happy?"

"I've been happy," Sophia protested only to realize the happiest she'd been in years were the weeks they'd spent together in St. Louis.

"When you moved to Chicago, why didn't you get another job in retail?"

Sophia mentally recoiled at the idea. After what happened at The Hope Chest…was Jake right? Had she refused to go after what she really wanted because she couldn't let go of the past?

"When I moved to Chicago to live with Theresa, she introduced me to a friend who got me an interview with a domestic service. It was close to the holidays, and they had a dozen or so corporate parties where bartenders and servers were needed, and half their staff was either on vacation or had come down with the flu."

Sophia swallowed. "During the interview, when they asked about past work experience, I told them I didn't have any. It wasn't a lie, exactly, since I never had done that kind of work before, and I was afraid no one would want to hire me after what happened here. But they were desperate enough that I don't know if it would have made a difference. I had one if not two jobs a night that first month, and before long, the only work history that mattered was what I'd done in Chicago."

Just the way she'd wanted it.

"By the time the position opened at the Dunworthys, I had plenty of references, from the agency where I'd worked for two years and from their clients, too. Maybe it wasn't the job of my dreams, but it let me forget."

"To forget that you had dreams?" he asked softly.

"Jake—"

"Close your eyes, Sophia. Go on, close them." When she'd reluctantly complied, he said, "When you picture yourself happy, what do you see?"

Staying in Clearville…working with Hope at the shop…Jake at her side…the two of them raising her child together.…

With each image, the ache in her heart grew until it hurt to draw breath. Sophia snapped her eyes open, banishing the longing. She pushed away from the sofa and ignored the knowing look in Jake's eyes. "Some dreams are impossible."

Maybe it was all Jake's talk of dreams, but by the time Sophia closed up the shop and headed home, she needed a dose of reality. She needed some concrete steps laid out before her so she could make sure she kept her feet on the ground right where they belonged.

Her mother was in the kitchen, preparing a late supper, but Sophia had slipped away to her room to make a phone call. She hadn't heard from Christine since leaving St. Louis, and she needed an update on how the plans were coming for her friend's business. Had she made an offer on the space she'd found? And what about the van she'd seen online, the one Christine thought might work for transporting food to all the events they'd soon be catering?

That was where Sophia needed to focus her attention, not on impossible dreams that didn't have a chance of coming true. But almost as soon as she reached her friend, Sophia realized *her* dreams weren't the only ones to go up in smoke.

"I'm so sorry, Sophia." Regret and disappointment dragged at her friend's words, making her normally upbeat and sunny voice almost unrecognizable. "I've be meaning to call, but I just didn't know how to tell you. I know you were counting on this job—counting on *me*."

"Christine, stop!" The last thing Sophia wanted was for her friend to add guilt to the load of heartache she was carrying. "I don't want you worrying about me. You have enough on your mind already."

Christine's father had been injured in a car accident and, while he expected to make a full recovery, he would be out of work for some time, a serious financial blow since he was self-employed. Not working meant not bringing home a paycheck, and Christine's mother couldn't take the risk of quitting her own job to be a part-time bookkeeper and babysitter now.

With everything going on, Christine had decided to put her own plans on hold while she helped out her parents as much as she could. "I'm not giving up," she vowed. "I still want to run my own business more than anything. This isn't going to stop me."

That sounded more like the Christine Sophia

knew—positive and determined—but as she hung up the phone, Sophia couldn't help feeling more than a little depressed. Okay, a catering company wasn't her dream, but the job had been a step forward, a move in the right direction toward her goal of ▪ finding a small place for herself and her baby in Chicago.

When you picture yourself happy, what do you see?

Funny how a tiny apartment in Chicago hadn't shown up in that picture at all.

"How was your first day back at the store?" Vanessa asked as Sophia stepped into the kitchen to give her mother a hand with dinner.

"How was my day…" Sophia mused.

On one hand, she'd had a decent sales tally based on what she recalled from five years ago. And she'd spent her free time sketching out a new layout to include Hope's latest finds into the already crowded store. On the other hand…

"Pretty good considering I'd only been there three hours before the cops showed up."

Vanessa rolled her eyes as she handed Sophia

a cucumber and a celery stalk for the salad to go with the spaghetti sauce simmering on the stove. The scent of oregano and garlic filled the kitchen and started Sophia's stomach growling.

"A simple misunderstanding," her mother insisted.

Sophia opened her mouth, ready to argue that Marlene Leary hadn't *misunderstood* anything when Jake's voice rang in her thoughts.

When is it okay for you to forget about the past? When is it your turn to be happy?

Was Jake right? Was she holding onto a past everyone—aside from Amy's parents—had already let go?

She'd left Clearville thinking it was best for everyone, and she'd carried those last memories of hurt, guilt and betrayal to Chicago. But the truth was, life in Clearville had gone on without her. The town had witnessed other scandals, weathered newer storms of gossip. Not that anyone had forgotten, but maybe those dark days loomed larger in her mind than they did anywhere else.

"Maybe you're right," she finally told her

mother as she pulled a knife from the drawer and started chopping vegetables on the built-in cutting board. "And for a first day, it was a good one."

She would need more good days before she could completely wipe all the negative memories from her mind or feel like she'd repaid Hope for the damage she'd done...but time was running out. Her parents' party was only a few days away, and her plan had always been to leave as soon as she spilled the whole truth about her job, Todd, the baby...and Jake.

"Sophia, is everything all right?"

Dragging her thoughts away from Jake, she briefly met her mother's concerned gaze before giving the vegetables all the attention of a surgeon performing a life-saving procedure. "What do you mean?"

"You and Jake." Vanessa finished washing the lettuce and dried her hands with slow, deliberate movements, her too-sharp gaze focused on Sophia.

Speculation filled her mother's voice, and

Sophia froze. She should have realized she couldn't pull this off. She could fool her father, her brothers—sometimes she feared she was on her way to fooling herself—but her mother had always read her so well.

"I know you both have only been here for a few days," Vanessa began, "but it's easy to see how he feels."

Sophia leaned against the counter in a mix of relief and confusion. "You think *Jake's* easy to read?" She'd thought so, too, when he was the Jake Cameron she met in St. Louis. But the Jake she knew now had her tiptoeing on the rugged coastline, unsure of her step along the slippery rocks, cautiously anticipating the next surprise wave ready to knock her off her feet.

"I think it's obvious he's crazy about you."

Worried nerves suddenly transformed into hopeful butterflies. It was frightening how much she wanted to believe that, but she'd believed in and been fooled by Jake before. She'd fallen for his sexy charm, and even though she'd gotten to know the real Jake Cameron over the past few days, his actions—his rejection—spoke louder than her mother's words.

And yet, Vanessa had raised three boys. Sam, most of all, had tried to get away with anything and everything. Somehow, though, she had always been two steps ahead of her sons at every turn.

Would Jake be able to fool her mother, or was Vanessa seeing a truth Sophia was afraid to trust?

"What isn't so obvious," her mother added, "is how you feel about him."

Vanessa set the towel aside, her hands completely still as she waited for Sophia's response. In an emotional rush, Sophia realized how much she'd missed sitting in this very kitchen, surrounded by her mother's mouthwatering cooking, pouring her heart out. She's missed her mother's sage advice as much as she'd missed her homemade meals.

In her teenage years, she'd made the mistake of letting her friends like Amy become a bigger influence. *Like replacing a home-cooked dinner with fast food,* Sophia thought. Quick and easy solutions that lacked any substance.

Hungry for her mother's point of view, Sophia confessed, "I want to trust Jake. I want to trust how I feel about him, but—I'm afraid."

"Love is one of the scariest emotions around, and people who find and hold on to true love are some of the bravest." Vanessa smiled. "But you're my adventurous girl, so it wouldn't surprise me at all to find out you've taken up the challenge."

Brave. Adventurous. Sophia wished she still lived up to those descriptions. "I'm not sure I want to where Jake is concerned."

"Why would you say that, Sophia?"

The truth she'd been hiding for so long pressed against her chest, and she simply couldn't keep it inside any longer. At least, not all of it.

"He says he's not a family man," Sophia confessed. Worse things could be said about a man, but to the Pirellis, family meant everything.

Vanessa frowned as Sophia expected she would, but her argument wasn't one Sophia thought she would make. "I talked to Sam and Drew. They said Jake did a great job with the ramp at Hope's house. He fit right in just like he has here. And Hope couldn't stop singing his praises."

"I know Jake wanted to help."

"And isn't that what family is all about? Supporting each other? Lending a hand when it's needed? Being there for each other?"

Jake *had* fit into her family easily enough that Sophia was tempted to believe he could be a permanent fixture instead of a temporary fix. But that wasn't what Jake wanted. He'd given her fair warning, and how foolish would she have to be to hope for more?

Almost as foolish as falling in love with him in the first place.

"I can't make him—" *love me* "—be someone he's not."

"And Jake says he's not a family man?" At Sophia's miserable nod, Vanessa asked, "But what does your heart say?"

Sophia thought of Jake as a young boy, losing

his mother's affection to his cold and distant stepfather, as a teenager, searching for a connection with his father only to find heartbreak instead. Was it any wonder, as an adult, he'd turned his back on the very idea of family? A word that meant love and caring and happiness in her life offered only rejection and disappointment in his.

"My heart tells me Jake wants a family more than any man I've ever known." Sophia crossed her arms over her stomach, cradling the tiny life growing inside. She swallowed hard. "But I don't know."

She might not have loved Todd, but she'd believed he was someone she could trust, someone she could count on, and not the kind of person who would throw all the blame at her feet and walk away, the same way Amy had years earlier.

And the stakes were so much higher now. What if she could convince Jake to give family life a try? What if they settled into that life together, and days, weeks or *months* from now Jake realized what he'd said all along was true.

How devastated would she be if he walked away then?

"I've been wrong before," she confessed.

"But what if you *aren't* wrong?" her mother countered. "What if Jake is exactly the man your heart thinks he is and you don't give him that chance? How much more will that loss hurt the both of you?"

Chapter Ten

As Jake walked into the living room the following evening, Vince Pirelli looked up from the book he was reading. Eyeing the younger man with amusement from above a pair of half glasses, he advised, "You might as well take a seat." He waved at the couch facing his recliner. "Having a wife and daughter has taught me many things about women. First of all that they are never ready when they say they'll be ready."

Jake fought a smile. Vince's statement might not have been the most politically correct, but he could testify to its accuracy. Normally, that kind of tardiness would have driven him crazy.

But with Sophia…the times while he waited for her to finish getting ready for a date were some of his favorite moments. Her slightly embarrassed apology while she rushed around her cousin's apartment seeking out misplaced keys, missing shoes, the tickets for the game they were attending. She'd been adorably flustered, and Jake had been constantly tempted to reach for her and make her forget all about what she was looking for so they could both concentrate on what they found in each other's arms.

"One thing I've learned," Jake told Vince, "is that your daughter is well worth the wait."

The older man nodded his approval. "I want you to make sure Sophia has a good time tonight."

"I will," Jake vowed, having already made that promise to himself when Sophia asked if he wanted to go to a birthday party for a friend of her brothers'.

The invitation had taken him completely by

surprise, something that must have shown as he stopped in the middle of clearing the dinner dishes from the table. Giving a self-conscious laugh, she said, "Debbie invited us, and I thought it would be fun. I'd like to promise you that at no time will the sheriff be called, but I'm afraid I can't."

The combination of doubt and determination in her brown eyes grabbed hold of something inside Jake. He'd asked Sophia earlier that day what she saw when she pictured herself happy, and Jake knew he had his own answer in the hint of her smile. Whatever made Sophia happy…

"Maybe we should swing by Bonnie's Bakery and get some doughnuts just in case," he'd said, and Sophia's laugh had washed over him. He hadn't enjoyed the sound of someone else's laughter so much since his time with Josh…

"I worry about her, you know." Vince sighed, pulling Jake from his memories and back to the conversation. "I've got my three boys living within a few miles of home, but my little girl's thousands of miles away." His dark eyes lasered into Jake, as if judging whether or not he could count on the younger man to shoulder some of that weight. "Doesn't seem right, you know?"

Jake struggled not to buckle under the pressure. He wanted more than to make Sophia happy for one night. He wanted to make sure Sophia and the baby she carried were happy for the rest of their lives, but he wasn't the man to promise that kind of happiness.

Face it, Jake, Mollie's words mocked him. *You aren't father material. How could you be? You never knew your real father, and you've never had any kind of relationship with your stepfather. What makes you think you'd be a better role model for Josh than his own flesh and blood?*

Because I love him as much as if he was my son.

He'd never said the words, never made the most gut-wrenching, most heartfelt argument he might have offered. Instead, he'd stood stoically by as Mollie excluded him from Josh's life, from the perfect family of father-mother-son where

Jake no longer had a place. Where he'd never had a place.

But what if Mollie was wrong? Maybe he hadn't fit into her ideal family, but might Sophia see things differently? Could there be room for him in a life with Sophia and her child? He'd never thought of himself as an artist, but in his years of surveillance, he'd discovered he was a decent photographer when he wasn't on the job snapping indecent photos. And like focusing on the perfect shot, Jake already pictured Sophia cradling her baby in her arms. If he pulled back, taking a wide angle, could he see himself included in that family portrait?

From the moment he'd found out Sophia was pregnant, he'd been putting up walls to keep Sophia from breaking into his heart, but he'd failed miserably. Probably because she was already there and had been from the moment they met.

Stop fighting so hard. It's okay to let someone close enough to care about you.

But despite the unspoken promise in Sophia's

words that she might be the one if he let her in, Jake couldn't give up the battle so easily.

Evading Vince's well-aimed question, Jake finally answered, "Sophia's stronger than you think. She's been through a lot, and she's learned to take care of herself."

"She's my little girl. I'm supposed to take care of her. Sometimes…" Vince shook his head. "It's easy to feel like I failed."

"Sophia loves you." Knowing he might well be crossing a line, Jake pointed out, "But she feels like she's the one who's let you down. That it was her fault you quit your job."

"I quit my job because I refused to keep quiet and work for a family telling lies about my daughter." Vince surged out of the easy chair as if propelled by his convictions. "I'd do the same thing again in a heartbeat, and it's turned out for the best like I knew it would. Retirement's given me the chance to do some work around the house, to fill in if my sons need a hand, and to spend more time with my wife. Just last year, Vanessa and I took a long overdue vacation to

Napa." He pointed to a picture on the mantel of himself and his wife, glasses of red wine raised in a toast, surrounded by oak barrels. "We've even talked about going to Italy, to see where my grandparents were born."

Jake watched Vince closely, looking for any sign of sorrow or regret, but all he saw was a man at peace with himself and his family, a man looking forward to the future. The only one dwelling on the past seemed to be Sophia. He'd sensed that since meeting the Pirellis. But had this trip home been enough to convince Sophia?

"Does Sophia know that the two of you want to travel?"

"Not sure if she does. Maybe not."

"You should tell her," Jake insisted. "Not that I know best when it comes to how to deal with your daughter, but Sophia—she feels like she's like a bit of an outsider. The only one who left home... I think she'd appreciate knowing that you and your wife are looking outside Clearville's boundaries, even if it's just for a vacation."

Vince nodded. "I will. And thanks," the older man added gruffly.

Uncomfortable with Vince's gratitude, Jake said, "Hey, it's just a thought."

"It's more than just that." The older man clapped Jake on the shoulder. "You got Sophia to come back, and I can't thank you enough for that, son."

Son. He had given up on being any man's son a long time ago, but with the warmth and weight of Vince's hand on his shoulder, Jake didn't think the word could have meant more to him coming from his own father.

"I'm a little surprised you wanted to go tonight," Jake said as he guided Sophia toward his rental car.

The touch of his hand was more heat than pressure on the small of her back, but without it, she would have likely raced back into her parents' house. The night was cool and overcast, the moon and stars cloaked by hazy clouds while the safety of the front porch light beckoned. But she forced herself to put one foot in front of the other as she walked toward Jake's rental car.

"Do you remember what you said that first day we were in town?" she asked. "When Mr. Whintner, who happens to be very good friends with the Learys, was shooting us dirty looks at the souvenir shop? You said we could leave right away or we could stay a while just to piss him off."

"I remember. So…you're planning on pissing people off tonight?"

"No," Sophia managed a small laugh. "At least I hope not. But ever since the break-in at Hope's shop, I feel like I've been hiding. I hardly left my room those final weeks before I graduated and left town. Once I got to Chicago it was easy to disappear, and even then, I took jobs where I supposed to be invisible."

And as much as she liked Christine and wished her friend well with her dream of opening her catering company, Sophia knew, for her, the job would have been more of the same—another position where she would have simply disappeared behind a uniform, losing a little more of herself every day until there wouldn't be anything left.

Reaching the passenger-side door, Sophia turned to face Jake. His palm slid from her back to her hip, and she had to force herself to concentrate on his words. "You could never be invisible. Not to me."

The husky murmur of his voice weakened her knees even more. "But I have been hiding," she argued even though she'd rather disappear into Jake's arms than show up at a party. "Even here with my family, I've been hiding the truth... I don't want to do that anymore."

Just like she didn't want a pretend relationship with a pretend boyfriend anymore. Each too-quick beat of her heart seemed to hasten the moment until they wouldn't *have* to pretend anymore. What would happen then? Where would the truth leave them? She needed to know if what she felt for Jake might be something real, something lasting...if there was a chance he might change his mind and decide he could be a family man after all....

The faint moonlight was as unrevealing as Jake's voice as he asked, "So you're ready to tell them everything?"

"Yes. I still want to wait until after the party, but I'm ready."

"You know your parents are going to be thrilled to have another grandchild to love and to spoil rotten."

Was it her imagination or had Jake's hand moved ever so slightly? Coming forward to brush against the barely-there swell of her baby bump that her high-waisted black dress hid from sight but not from touch?

"And you're going to be a wonderful mother."

This time there was no mistaking the stroke of his thumb across her belly in a touch so tender, yet so seductive, her entire body trembled. "Jake…"

She tried to say more, but her voice caught, and the one word was all she could manage. The name of the only man who could leave her weak in the knees and break her heart at the same time.

"And this little kid," he started, his voice so rough he had to clear his throat before he added, "he's gonna be so lucky to have you."

But would Sophia be lucky enough to have *Jake?*

Couldn't he see he'd left a spot open in the picture he'd painted? A place only he could fill?

Afraid he'd pull away if she pressed too hard, Sophia clung to the moment, to the tenuous connection of Jake's hand cradling her unborn baby. "So you think it's a boy, too?" she whispered.

"Yeah, a little boy with dark eyes like his mother..."

Not the icy blue of his father.

Jake didn't have to say the words for Sophia to know they were there. Right between them where she feared they always would be. The tightrope she felt she'd been walking narrowed to a razor's edge, the blade already cutting deep. The ache of it burned behind her eyelids and scalded her throat. But maybe the old saying was true—maybe this too would make her stronger. "Something else that being here has helped me figure out—I can't change the past. And I don't want to. I want this baby, Jake," she insisted, her voice breaking on his name and the knowledge of how much she wanted *him,* too. "Boy or girl. Brown eyes or blue, I *love* this baby."

"I know you do."

"But it's too much, isn't it?"

Too much to expect Jake, who'd already warned her he wasn't a family man, to even consider a real relationship with a woman carrying another man's child. But just when she thought Jake would pull away, when she'd already braced for the loss of his hand, her lone support on that teetering edge, he slid both arms around her waist. Pulling her tight until her baby was sheltered between them.

"This baby is part of you. Boy or girl. Brown eyes or blue," he echoed. "That's all that matters."

Sophia thought there might have been a time or two in her life when she'd been less inclined to spend a few hours with a rowdy birthday crowd, but she couldn't think of a single one as she followed Jake through the crowd at Sullivan's Bar. A baseball game and sports highlights played on the overhead televisions while eighties rock blared from the jukebox. The stage in the corner, reserved for a house band or karaoke, was blessedly empty, but a microphone stand under a lone spotlight stood at the ready.

Jake shot an apologetic look over his shoulder before he leaned close to shout, "I'm trying to find a table."

"Don't bother. This place is always packed, and on a night like tonight..."

On a night like tonight, Sophia wanted to be somewhere quiet and intimate. That same desire shone in Jake's eyes, and as their gazes locked, the crowd, the televisions and the music all faded away, and for a moment, only the two of them existed.

"We were wondering if the two of you would make it." Sam clapped Jake on the shoulder, breaking into their insular world and letting the bar's noisy atmosphere rush back in.

"I'm always up for a good party."

"Me, too, man," her brother agreed, missing the wry tone behind the words and the look she and Jake shared.

"Where's the guest of honor?" Sophia asked, unable to spot Billy Cummings, the sheriff's son, in the crowd.

"Over there." Drew pointed to a group of guys gathered around blond-haired Billy near the polished walnut and brass-trimmed bar. A cheer went up as they raised their glasses in a toast and Billy downed a long drink.

"Looks like he's having a good time."

"You know Billy. Any reason to party. Speaking of parties, are we all set for Mom and Dad's?" Drew asked.

"I think so. You're taking them out to tour the newest house you're building, so that should give us plenty of time to set up the tables and decorations. Sam, you'll be there to help, right?" At his nod, she added, "I ordered the cake today, and I'm going to call Rolly's to give the final head count for the food tomorrow before I go into work at The Hope Chest."

She took a deep breath and exhaled on a sigh of relief as she realized how close they were to pulling off this surprise. "I don't think Mom and Dad suspect a thing. They're going to be so excited. But—"

"But what?" Jake asked. "Sounds like you've thought of everything."

"Everything except a present," she confessed guiltily. "I was going to mail them a gift from St. Louis, but once I decided to make the trip home, I thought I'd find something here. So far, I'm coming up empty."

"You know just being here is the best present you could give them," Drew said, giving her the all-knowing big brother gaze.

"I know they're glad I'm home—"

"Ecstatic is more like it," Sam chimed in.

"They worry, you know."

Yeah, she knew. The sinking feeling was all too familiar.

"But you've changed, little sis. I can see it, and I'm sure the folks can, too."

The acknowledgement wasn't something she expected or was even 100 percent sure she believed. "I—you really think so?"

"Just coming back here and facing the past shows you've changed. Add in all you've done for the anniversary party and going back to work at The Hope Chest..." Drew shrugged. "You've grown up."

Sam sighed. "I suppose this means I can't call you Fifi anymore, huh?"

Touched by her brothers' words, Sophia gave a watery laugh. "You know, I think I'd miss it if you stopped."

Her brothers shared a look, wrapped her in a group hug and took turns saying, "Welcome home, Fifi! We've missed you, Fifi!"

Laughing at their antics, Sophia couldn't remember when she'd last felt so carefree. Probably not since the time when she hadn't minded being her big brothers' little sister—their Fifi. Amid the teasing, Sophia caught Jake's eye. This was what he wanted for her and her baby. Not her family's protection because she couldn't take care of herself, but their laughter and their love. And it was everything she wanted for Jake, too. Everything she could give Jake if only he would let her.

"I've missed you guys, too, and I'm glad to be home."

Home, a word that would always mean Clearville for Sophia. But she pushed that realization aside for now. "We do still need to come up with a present for Mom and Dad, though."

"Nick was talking about the three of us going in together. Might as well be the four of us instead," Sam suggested.

"What are you getting them?"

Drew huffed a sigh. "That's still up for debate. We can't agree on anything."

"I told you I know a guy who has a vintage bike like the one Dad had when he was a teenager—"

"Forget about the motorcycle, Sam," Drew cut in with an exasperation that told Sophia her brothers had had this argument many times before. "Anyway, assuming the four of us can agree, we'll all pitch in."

"I don't suppose Nick's coming tonight?" Her oldest brother's presence always added an element of tension, but Sophia worried about the way he'd secluded himself and Maddie since the divorce.

Sam shook his head. "Nope. It's getting harder and harder to drag him away from that hole."

"Hey, I helped him build that 'hole,'" Drew protested, referring to the cabin outside of town he and Nick had built as one of Drew's first construction projects.

"You did too good of a job. Maybe if Nick wasn't so comfortable sitting at home, we'd see him out more."

"Way I see it, Nick's gotta start taking some responsibility for his own misery. We all feel bad for the way things ended with Carol, but it's not our fault." Drew's gaze singled out Sophia as he repeated, "Nick doesn't have the right to take his anger out on you, Sophia. We should have made that clear a long time ago, and I'm sorry we didn't. You made a choice to leave, but no way does that make you anything like his ex. Right, Sam?"

Caught up in watching a grand slam replay on a screen above the bar, Sam rejoined the conversation with a distracted, "Never said it did…"

"But we never said it *didn't*," Drew stressed.

"Huh?"

Her youngest brother's confusion was enough to make Sophia feel like she'd stepped into a comedy skit. Still, she found their somewhat clumsy, yet endearing support touching and leaned forward to give them each another hug. "Thank you both. Now, go have a good time."

"Only if you do the same," Drew stipulated.

Sam gave in a little easier. "First round's on me!" he called as he grabbed Drew and pulled him toward the bar.

"You should go," she told Jake. "Knowing Sam and Drew, they'll expect you to buy one of the rounds whether you're drinking or not, so you might as well."

He hesitated for a moment before saying, "Maybe I'll have a beer. Do you want anything?"

"Just a sparkling water."

Sophia had a good idea that Jake had played a part in her brothers' sudden apology, much in the same way her dad used to make them shake hands as kids and say sorry after one fight or another.

"Families are forever," Vince would say, *"so you might as well learn to like each other."*

Families are forever…she'd taken that for granted growing up. Had even foolishly distanced herself from the people closest to her, knowing all along they would be waiting for her when she finally came home.

Jake had never had that sense of security. She could see how perfectly he fit into her family, but childhood had taught him he couldn't trust that closeness. When he'd told her how the search for his father ended in tragedy, the pain and resignation in his eyes revealed that he'd given up on finding the family he wanted. Jake couldn't change his past anymore than she could change her own, but was there a chance that *she* could change *his* mind about a family in his future?

Chapter Eleven

Sophia watched as the crowd around the bar seemed to part as Jake neared. Dressed in charcoal-colored slacks and a slate-blue dress shirt, he looked amazing. The sleeves were rolled back to reveal tanned, muscular forearms and a stainless-steel watch on his left wrist. Amid a sea of T-shirts and blue jeans, he moved with a confident ease.

With his attention centered on the bartender, she had the chance to study the way his hair gleamed like aged gold in the overhead lighting, the way his rugged features made his face just shy of perfect, the way the corner of his mouth kicked up at some silly thing Sam said.

Todd had taught her that no matter how expensive, style could never add up to substance, but with Jake, Sophia had learned the deeper she looked, the more she would find.

This baby is part of you. That's all that matters.

Sophia was frightened by how desperately she was clinging to those words—like dangling over a hundred-foot drop by threadbare rope— hoping she wasn't reading more into them than she should.

"Definitely a billboard." Recognizing Debbie Mattson's voice, Sophia turned to find the blonde gazing at Jake with comically lovesick sigh. "Full color. Full…everything," she teased. "You are a lucky, lucky woman, Sophia Pirelli."

"I'd have to agree. Having Jake here has been amazing."

In a matter of days, he'd become such a part of her life, Sophia didn't know if she would ever look around her hometown again without picturing him there. She never would have gone to the party without Jake by her side. She likely wouldn't have agreed to work at Hope's shop.

As if picking up on the turn in Sophia's thoughts, Debbie said, "I heard you had some excitement at The Hope Chest after you left the bakery this afternoon." She leaned closer, although Sophia doubted anyone could hear much of anything over the music and laughter. "I saw Marlene Leary and some of her followers lined up like crows on a fence, all beady-eyed and preening to one another as they watched. Wouldn't surprise me if she was the one to call the sheriff in the first place."

"The thought did cross my mind," Sophia admitted. Her mother may have believed it was all a misunderstanding, but Debbie didn't seem to have any doubt.

"Marlene's been out to get Hope for years."

"Out to get Hope?" Sophia blinked, startled by the certainty in Debbie's words. Sophia had been the target of Marlene's wrath, going back to the days after the break-in—the break-in at

Hope's shop. Sophia had always known she'd given Amy a golden opportunity, but had the location been something more than easy pickings? "But why would Marlene be out to get Hope?"

Debbie raised her glass in a *who knows?* gesture. "Bad blood between the two of them for some reason."

Bad blood. Had some of it spilled over, fueling Amy's scheme?

"Look, don't worry about any of that tonight. You have a good time while the rest of us single women drool with envy."

Sophia was still chuckling at Debbie's parting line when Jake made his way back to her side, a bottle of beer and glass of ice water in hand. "What's so funny?"

"You've got a fan in Debbie. Play your cards right, you might get free doughnuts for life."

"Hmm." Jake set his beer and her water on a nearby table. "Tempting, but not as tempting as this…"

Ignoring the people gathered at the bar, he

leaned close and brushed his lips against hers. Once, twice…

Each barely-there pass made her long for more—more pressure, more passion, more *Jake.*

The crowd surged around them, bumping Sophia closer to Jake, and he wrapped a protective arm around her. "How about we go outside? The patio's pretty much empty."

At Sophia's nod, they made their way toward the side door. Jake was reaching for the handle when the door swung out and a young woman rushed inside.

"Oops, sorry!" she apologized, and Jake did a double-take, barely recognizing Kayla Walker. The new mother wore enough makeup to give the impression she was actually old enough to be in a bar, and her blond hair tumbled around her shoulders.

"Jake! Sophia! I should have known you'd be here tonight. Seems like the whole town has shown up."

"You look amazing," Sophia said. "Has Annabel started sleeping through the night?"

"Even better!" Kayla glowed as she laughed for no reason. "There's someone I want you to meet, and as soon as you do, you'll see why I'm so happy."

She caught the arm of a thin young man with bleach-blond hair beneath a backward baseball cap and brown eyes identical to Annabel's. "Sophia, Jake, this is Devon Dees," Kayla announced with a flourish that whipped the rug right out from beneath Jake's feet.

Devon, the father of Kayla's baby. The man Kayla had sworn she never wanted to see again, and the man Sophia had insisted the other woman still loved. Judging by the way Kayla locked her arms around the man's waist and rested her head against his chest, Sophia had been dead-on.

Barely aware of the conversation going on around him, Jake still picked up a few key words—marriage, father, family. He thought he might have managed a few appropriate responses before Sophia made their excuses and he made his escape onto the patio.

Leaving the noisy, crowded bar, Jake sucked

in a gulp of fresh air. His ears rang in the almost overwhelming silence. Maybe he should have stayed inside where the music and laughter had a chance of drowning out the doubts raging through his thoughts.

"Jake, is something wrong?" Sophia asked, following him to the far end of the patio where he'd braced his hands against the wrought iron railing.

"You called that one, didn't you?"

"What do you mean?" Her expression a bit wary, she stopped just shy of standing by his side.

"Even after everything Kayla said that day at the farmhouse, you knew. You knew she wanted Devon back."

"It was obvious she still loved him."

Thoughts of his relationship with Mollie swirling through his mind, Jake argued, "No, it wasn't! What was *obvious* was everything she said about never wanting to see him again, about not taking him back even if he came crawling… that was obvious."

"Kayla was hurt and angry. She said some things she didn't mean. Couples fight, but then they make up. It happens."

"Yeah." It certainly did...

"Wait a minute." Realization dawned in Sophia's expression, anger sparking in her dark eyes. "You don't think that *I'm* waiting for Todd to come after me, do you? That after what he did, I'd take him back?"

Jake wanted to deny it. He wanted the whole idea to be as ridiculous as she made it sound. "It happens."

"Just because Kayla and Devon got back together—"

"Not them. Me," Jake interrupted. "It happened to me when my fiancée went back to her ex-husband."

Even in the patio's dim lighting, Jake saw her face pale. Too late Jake remembered Todd Dunworthy had a fiancée, too, one he failed to tell Sophia about. "Ex-fiancée," he quickly clarified. "Our relationship is over."

"Is it? Because if either of us still has feelings for an ex, I'd say it's you, Jake. Not me."

He started to protest, denials that pretty much echoed Sophia's, and he realized he was likely acting like a total ass. "I don't have feelings for Mollie. Not anymore, but…"

"But what?"

"She has a son. Josh." He had yet to figure out how simply saying the boy's name could make him happy and make him hurt all at the same time. "I loved—I *love* that kid."

"A son? She—how old is he?" Sophia asked, even though he could read a dozen other questions circling in her wide eyes.

"He's six. He was a year old when his parents separated and two when Mollie and I met. She was divorced by then and quick to tell everyone—including me—how glad she was to be rid of her husband."

"When did that change?"

Jake gave a rough laugh. "I honestly don't know how to answer that. On one hand, I felt blindsided when Mollie told me she was getting back together with Roger. But on the other hand, I wonder if she was in love with him the whole three years we were together."

"You were together for three years?"

He heard the shock in Sophia's voice. "Surprised I lasted that long?"

"You're the one who said you weren't a family man, Jake! Now you're telling me that you were engaged, that you were a part of a little boy's life, and one short trip down the aisle from being a stepfather. So don't blame me if this has taken me by surprise."

Sophia was right; he had sprung this on her with no warning. But everything about his relationship with Mollie left him feeling defensive. "You're right. I'm sorry." Determined to finish what he'd started with as little emotion as possible, he said, "I suppose I should have realized something was wrong with our relationship when Mollie couldn't settle on a wedding date."

There'd been other hints, too, mostly to do with Jake's involvement with Josh. At the time, he'd taken Mollie's determination to see to all of Josh's daily needs as a single mother's over-protectiveness. He should have questioned her attempts to keep him on the sidelines, but then again, the position was one Jake was used to after all the years he'd spent as an outsider in his own home while growing up.

"I wrote it off as cold feet and didn't think anything of it. Then one day she had a fender bender coming home from work. She was already late getting Josh from daycare, so when she called, I told her I'd do it. No big deal. Only it turned out to be a very big deal because I wasn't on the list of people approved to pick him up."

Mollie had sworn it was an oversight; after all, Josh had only started school a few weeks earlier, and she simply hadn't thought Jake would need to pick the boy up. But Mollie wasn't the type to forget even the smallest detail, especially not when it came to her son.

"I told her I wanted a bigger part in Josh's life after that. I wanted my name on that damn list, and I wanted to take him to a ballgame and to go to the movies and teach him to ride a bike—"

Jake' voice cut out, and he swallowed hard, wishing for the beer he'd left indoors.

"Did Mollie agree?"

"Not without a bit of a fight, but yeah, she gave in."

Jake could still picture Josh grinning up at him from beneath the Dodgers cap he bought for him and the delight the boy had taken in tossing peanut shells on the ground instead of in a garbage can. And the cartoon they'd seen so many times in the theater both he and Josh could practically recite the entire movie.

Dammit, he should have stuck to baseball games and movies! But Josh had wanted the bike so bad…

"A few months before his fifth birthday, Josh started hinting around that he wanted a bike. A *real* bike, not some little bike for babies. I figured, why not? All boys have bikes, right? I told him I'd teach him how to ride and he'd be cruising the neighborhood in no time.

"It never occurred to me Mollie would disagree, but she flat-out refused. She said I'd overstepped by promising Josh a bike without talking to her first. I accused her of being too overprotective again. I was sure that once Josh learned how to ride, she'd see how safe it was and would realize she'd overreacted. So I bought him the bike a few weeks before his birthday."

"Oh, Jake."

"Stupid, I know, and it only gets worse. A week before his birthday, I took Josh out for his first lesson. He was going great and having a blast when—somehow one of the training wheels got stuck in a crack in the sidewalk. The bike pitched to the side, and Josh fell over with it.

"I couldn't get there fast enough, but at the same time, watching him fall was like being stuck in one of those slow-motion nightmares where everything moves like it's underwater."

And that was exactly how he'd felt—trapped, suffocating, unable to breathe—when he saw that Josh wasn't crying, wasn't moving, wasn't conscious despite the helmet meant to protect him. The call to Mollie to tell her to meet him at the hospital was the worst he hoped he'd ever have to make.

"But Josh was okay," Sophia stated as if refusing to accept any other outcome.

Reaching out, he pulled her into his arms, taking comfort in the warmth and softness of her body fitted perfectly against his own. "Yeah," he said, gruffly, inhaling the strawberry scent of her shampoo. "He was okay. But they had to run tests and keep him overnight for observation."

At which time the nurse had informed him visiting hours were over and he would have to leave as only family was allowed to stay past that time. Family being Mollie and her ex-husband, Roger.

"I should have realized then there was no way Mollie would forgive me—"

"Jake, it was an accident. Accidents and kids go hand in hand!"

He heard what Sophia was saying, but the words couldn't penetrate the scar tissue of guilt hardened around his heart. "I was trying so damn hard to prove that I could be a good father when the truth was, I didn't know what the hell

I was doing! I never knew my father. My stepfather was the worst example I could have when it came to parenting. Mollie was right when she said I didn't have what it took."

Listening to Jake, Sophia could feel her heart breaking, her hope for the future being torn apart by his rough words. All because of an accident. *One* accident.

"Mollie was wrong, Jake. Can't you see that? One accident doesn't mean you're a bad father. One accident doesn't mean anything! If I have a boy and he's anything like my brothers, I have no doubt he'll give me gray hair by the time he's two. He'll probably strip years off my life with crazy stunts, and I'll have to threaten to lock him away in his room until he's twenty-one. Just like my parents did with all three of my brothers!"

Uncertainty still filled Jake's gaze. Was it only wishful thinking that she was seeing a longing there, too? A desire to believe what she was saying? "I don't know, Sophia."

"But I do."

Thanks to her mother's love and patience and

her father's unflappable humor, kindness and integrity, Sophia had a lifetime of knowledge to draw from when it came to the right way to raise her son.

Knowledge Jake didn't have and knowledge his fiancée had used against him. Sophia felt a slow-burning anger starting to boil at the way the woman had struck where she'd known Jake to be the most vulnerable…

And yet hadn't Sophia done the same thing? Turning Jake's words about not being a family man against him that day at the creek? He'd hurt her when he pulled away, but instead of giving him the chance to explain, she'd lashed out, trying to hurt him, too.

"I'm so sorry, Jake," she said, apologizing as much for the pain she'd caused as for what his ex-fiancée had put him through.

Raucous laughter and an off-key rendition of "Happy Birthday" drifted out to the patio, reminders of the party still going strong inside. Jake's sigh stirred her hair as he said, "I promised to show you a good time tonight. Believe me when I say this was not what I had in mind."

"It's okay."

It might not have been a good time, but it was good to know what she was up against. Jake's past was a serious hurdle, but Sophia doubted he realized the most important part of what he'd told her.

I was trying so damn hard to prove that I could be a good father...

To be a good father to another man's child.

He might as well have reached into her chest and squeezed her heart. But that was no surprise. He'd held it in his hands practically from the moment they met. "Let's go back inside," she decided suddenly. "We'll tell Billy happy birthday and then we can go."

"Are you sure?"

Sophia smiled. "I'm sure."

Looking around the bar as they stepped back inside, Sophia spotted Billy at his spot near the bar. As the crowd mercifully ended their birthday serenade, he took an elaborate bow without spilling a drop, but Sophia could remember so many times when he and her brothers hadn't been nearly so careful.

After ordering an iced tea, Sophia held up her glass. "I'd like to offer a toast."

Her words went largely unnoticed by the raucous crowd, but before she could make a second subtle attempt, Sam let out a sharp whistle. "Hey, everybody, listen up!"

Just like that, she not only had Billy's attention, but the entire bar was staring at her. The music and laughter that had been so loud only moments before came to a stop. Or maybe it only seemed that way because the pulse pounding in her ears made hearing anything else impossible. Sophia did her best to ignore the way the crowd's attention crawled like bugs over her skin. If it had been up to her, she would have darted back into a darkened corner. But she wasn't doing this for herself.

She glanced over at Jake amid dozens of familiar faces, confusion and a bit of concern on his expression. "Now that I have everyone's attention, I, um, wanted to say that, growing up, we've all made our share of mistakes. And I think this would be a great time to toast some of Billy's memorable antics and to recall all the times his parents swore he would never make it to this, his thirtieth birthday!" The crowd laughed as Billy hung his head in mock shame. "And I'm sure my brothers have some great memories, too. We all know if they weren't involved in the actual event, they most likely instigated it!"

As Sam and Drew protested their innocence, Sophia said, "One stunt I remember is when you three decided to use the empty community pool as your own personal skate park."

"Hey, I almost landed that three-sixty," Sam argued.

"Instead you landed in the hospital with a broken arm," Sophia said wryly. She drew a laugh from the crowd, but her eyes were locked on Jake's.

"That's nothing!" Drew protested. "What about the time Billy tied his bike to the back of

his mom's van and rode behind her all the way
to town?"

"The only guy to get a ticket on a ten-speed!"

As Sam, Drew and Billy continued to outdo
each other with their often outrageous, sometimes dangerous stunts, Sophia tried to slip away
back to Jake's side. But before she'd made her
escape, Sam caught her by the arm. "Yeah, don't
think you're getting away that easily. Not until
you admit your part in all this."

"What part?"

"Who exactly told me I couldn't jump our front
fence with my bike?"

"You couldn't," Sophia argued, the same thing
she'd said as a know-it-all seven-year-old.

"Yeah, but after you said I couldn't, I had to
try."

And just like that, the tables turned with her
brothers and Billy pointing out all the times
Sophia and her friends had frequently witnessed
her brothers' mishaps after egging them on from
the sidelines. "So you're saying it was all my
fault?"

The three guys exchanged a look. "Yes."

Not long ago, Sophia would have fired back at her brothers, angry and embarrassed at the way they'd ganged up on her. Able to dish it out, but not willing to take it. But now, now she started to laugh. "If we'd known then we had that kind of power over you, just imagine what we could have made you do!"

"Hey, we never said you had *power* over us."

"Oh, but we made you do all those crazy things. Sounds like we were the ones in control," she shot back.

But no, Sophia didn't have power over them, they insisted. "Guys always do stupid things to impress the girl," Sam insisted. "It's a rule."

It might have been the rule, but it wasn't always guys who were out to do the impressing. Meeting Jake's golden gaze, she saw the pride in his gaze along with the awareness of what she'd done for him.

She might have started with the idea that she had something to prove to Jake, but she'd proved something to herself as well. If she was going to expect him to overcome the demons of his past, it was only fair that she face down some of her own.

Chapter Twelve

"I heard you had a good time last night."

Sophia looked away from the computer screen to meet her father's gaze as he stepped into the study. She'd been doing some research on Hope's newest pieces before heading into the shop, but she turned her attention away from antique lamps to offer a smile to her dad. "I'm glad Jake and I went," she said, skirting the truth a little. Finding out about Jake and his relationship with Josh—and Mollie—answered so many questions, but so many still remained.

Had everything she said last night been enough

for Jake to see that even the best, most vigilant parents couldn't keep kids from getting hurt? That the love he had for Josh said far more about his abilities as a father than his mistake in judgment did? That even though he thought he wasn't a family man, Sophia knew he was a man who needed a family?

And the more basic question—where had Jake gone when he left the house that morning?

His rental car was still parked out front, so Sophia knew he hadn't gone far. And while she wasn't surprised he might need some time alone after the emotional revelations the night before, she was a little disappointed.

"What are you working on?" Vince asked, drawing her attention back to the computer screen.

"Hope bought a truckload of furniture and artwork from an estate sale. I wanted to research some of the pieces. I think they might be antiques and pretty valuable."

When she'd phoned Hope to ask how she wanted the new items priced, her friend had responded with a blithe, *"Whatever you think they'll sell for."* It was not the answer Sophia had expected or a call she was prepared to make without a little more information.

"Hope's lucky to have you."

Sophia was the lucky one, having a second chance to make up for disappointing Hope in the past. She glanced back at the website she'd found, but the computer had already switched into a power save mode and a slideshow screen-saver flashed across the screen.

"Look at that, Sophia," Vince pointed to a photo of a vineyard. "I know it's early, but I can almost taste a fine, red wine just looking at that picture, can't you?"

"Is that Napa?" Her parents had vacationed there a few years ago, Sophia recalled, the only trip she could remember the two of them making without four kids in tow.

Affecting a wounded heart, Vince said, "Your nana must be rolling in her grave. That is the Pirelli motherland."

"Two generations removed," Sophia laughed.

"Three, I guess, counting Maddie." *And her own soon-to-be Pirelli grandchild.*

"I suppose you're right," her father sighed. "Still, it would be something to visit, to experience the history of the country and of our family."

Sophia cupped a hand beneath her chin to keep her jaw from dropping at the wistful tone in her father's voice. "So, you want to travel?"

"Hmm, once upon a time, I dreamed of moving to Italy."

This time, nothing could keep Sophia's shock from showing. "Seriously?"

Vince smiled. "Not to worry, sweetheart. I wasn't planning on up and leaving your mother and you kids. This was when I was in my teens, long before I was even dating your mom. I wasn't always an old man, you know."

"You're not old now!" Sophia protested.

The photo on the screen shifted, this time showing a sun-bleached fishing village on the Mediterranean coast. "Back then, I planned to travel all around Italy, but not as a tourist.

I figured I'd find some Pirelli relative I could move in with, and I'd learn all I needed to know from the best."

Amazed to realize her father had ever wanted to do anything other than live and work in the town where he'd been born, she asked, "What did you want to learn?"

"Anything and everything. I wanted to fish, to cook, to learn to make wine. The possibilities were endless." Reaching over, he jiggled the mouse; the screensaver disappeared, replaced by a background photo of their family. It was a candid shot Vince must have taken with Sam, Drew and Nick standing beside Sophia and her mother.

"And then I met your mother…"

Her father's voice trailed off, so Sophia filled in, "And you gave up your dreams."

"No, sweetheart. Not at all. I traded in one dream for another, and I've never regretted it. Not for a second." He looked around the room, but Sophia sensed he was taking stock of the entire house and the decades' worth of memories stored there. "But now that you and your brothers are all grown up, I think your mother and I would really like to have an adventure or two and see a bit more of the world."

So much for thinking *she* was the one with all the secrets! Her father's expression was completely calm as if he had no idea the kind of bombs he was dropping.

"I always felt you were a bit more like me that way," Vince mused. Suddenly he laughed. "Remember when we went to the ice cream shop, the one with all the different flavors, and you asked to try them all because—"

"How would I know which was my favorite unless I tasted each one?" Sophia finished the story she'd heard dozens of times over the years. Her smile fading away, she said, "But I thought you were frustrated with me for being unable to decide. Not about ice cream, but about what I wanted to do with my life."

Vince leaned a hip against the side of the desk. "With the boys, it was all so easy. They *knew.* From the time they were in diapers, they knew what they wanted to do, what made them happy. Your mother and I were never disappointed in you, sweetheart. But we did worry. That you wouldn't find the one, special thing that made you happiest. And then you started working at The Hope Chest. You'd come home from work filled with stories of the tourists you met, the merchandise you sold, whatever new, amazing find Hope had made. It was like listening to Nick, Drew and Sam talk about animals, tools, and cars."

Realizing her father was right and more conscious than ever of the opportunity she'd squandered, Sophia said, "You might have told me at the time I'd found my calling. I kept telling myself it was just a stupid after-school job my parents forced me to take."

"No, you didn't." At Sophia's look, Vince chuckled. "Okay, maybe you did, but your mother and I had learned that encouraging a teenager to do something was the surest way to guarantee they do the opposite."

"But I still screwed it up, didn't I?"

"Sophia…" Vince's dark brows knitted together as he held out his arms and pulled her into a hug. "You made a mistake, but it was a long time ago. Too long to still be carrying this guilt around."

"You quit your job because of me…" Her words were a muffled protest against his plaid shirt.

Her father pulled back to meet her gaze. "I quit my job because I couldn't keep quiet when the Learys tried to turn you into an outcast and blame you for something that wasn't your fault. But like I was telling Jake, everything happens for a reason."

"What does Jake have to do with this?"

"He suggested that I talk to you about wanting to travel and see the world outside of Clearville. But I think all this—" reaching up, he brushed a tear from her cheek "—is what he really wanted us to get out in the open." Vince smiled. "He's a good man, your Jake."

A good man? Yes. Hers? Oh, how Sophia wanted him to be. But she was running out of time to convince Jake that the only thing he didn't have as far as what it took to make him a family man was a family. And if he'd let her, she was more than willing to share her own.

At ten after six, Sophia flipped the sign in the store window to *Closed* and locked the front door. "Well done, my dear. I couldn't have managed better myself," Hope applauded as Sophia dropped with an exhausted sigh onto the settee across from the wheelchair.

A steady stream of customers had filled the shop most of the day, and when Hope had arrived unexpectedly after being dropped off by a friend, Sophia had felt a bit self-conscious, wondering if the shopkeeper was checking up on her.

But before long, Sophia realized Hope wasn't paying much attention to what she was doing. Instead, Hope had sat in her chair, chatting with tourists or friends who'd heard she was back at the shop and stopped by.

"I printed out what information I could find on

the pieces you bought at the estate sale." Sophia reached for the folder she'd set on the coffee table earlier. "You should really have it all appraised because I'm far from an expert, but I'm sure the lamps are Tiffany." She flipped through the pages, showing varying price ranges for items similar to Hope's latest finds.

"And the cradle..." To Sophia's embarrassment, the pinprick of tears welled behind her eyelids just as they had when she first saw the handmade baby bed. She'd been drawn to the cradle again and again during her free time. She'd dusted the narrow rails and every nook and cranny of the intricate carvings before she polished the rich oak to a luxurious shine. When she finished, she ran one hand across the curved headboard. Even though she still had to imagine her baby curled up on the rainbow print mattress, somehow touching the cradle made her pregnancy that much more real. That much more tangible....

And obvious, Sophia feared, as she realized she'd been humming a lullaby beneath her breath, her hand cradling her stomach, with Hope's too-observant gaze watching the whole time. Clearing her throat now, she said, "I couldn't find any identifying marks on it, so there's no way to know its history. But it's obviously a work of love, and well, I don't even know how to price something like that."

Hope reached for the folder, but to Sophia's surprise, she closed it and set it aside. "Thank you, Sophia." Despite the words, the woman's smile seemed somewhat wistful, sad even.

"Um, you're welcome." Hearing a hint of question in her own voice, she added, "It was fun to do the research."

"Not for that. Thank you for reminding me how this shop should be run. Watching you today, seeing your excitement dealing with the customers and the thought you've put into the new merchandise, it reminds me of myself when I first opened The Hope Chest, and it's made my decision easier."

"I don't understand. What decision?"

Maneuvering her wheelchair behind the

counter without answering the question, Hope took a box off a shelf. "Do you remember this?" she asked once she'd wheeled back beside Sophia and handed her the box.

Lifting the top and brushing aside a layer of tissue paper, Sophia's eyes widened when she saw the hand-carved jewelry box. Even without turning the key, she knew the tinny, familiar melody that would play. She'd had her eye on the velvet-lined box from the first time she saw it years ago. "You kept this? I thought for sure you would have sold it."

"I did," Hope confessed with a laugh, "once you'd left for Chicago. And then a few weeks ago, not long after I heard from your mother that you were coming home, I found this jewelry box, the same one from all those years ago, at a consignment shop. And I knew you were meant to have it. Just like I knew from the moment you started working here, you were meant to take over running this shop."

"I—what?" Thank goodness the jewelry box was resting on her lap or it might have slid from her nerveless fingers and fallen to the floor. "Run the store? When I started working here, I was still in high school. I only worked a few days a week!"

Even as she made the protest, she heard her father's voice. *We worried that you wouldn't find the one, special thing that made you happiest. And then you started working at The Hope Chest.*

"I noticed you still wear the ring you bought here. You went back and forth over whether you should buy it or not."

Sophia glanced down at the filigree band. "You said if it fit, I had to have it."

Reaching over, Hope gave Sophia's hand a squeeze. "It fits."

"I—I can't believe you want me to do this. After everything that happened—"

Hope shook her vehemently enough to almost dislodge the reading glasses from a top her head. "In the past. No reason to even mention it."

But Sophia couldn't let it go. Not when Hope

was offering her so much and she'd— "I never even said how sorry I was."

"Of course you did! That night, you stayed with me when you could have run off with Amy and her friends. I wouldn't have known you had any part in what happened, but you waited with me until the ambulance came. Over and over, you told me how sorry you were. I forgave you years ago, Sophia. I only wish you'd forgive yourself."

"I *had* to stay with you. It was all my fault in the first place, and saying sorry isn't nearly enough. You've already given me a second chance by letting me fill in these past few days—"

"No, no. That's not why I asked at all."

Seeing the distraught look on the woman's face, Sophia insisted, "I was more than willing. Anything to make up for what I did."

"Stop, please, Sophia. Just…stop." Hope closed her eyes for a brief moment and exhaled a sigh that seemed to sap her energy. "It wasn't your fault, and it wasn't Amy's fault either. Not really.

Not when…" Opening her eyes, she said, "It was our fault."

"Whose?"

"Mine…and Carl Leary's."

"I don't understand. What does Amy's father have to do with any of this?" Carl Leary had always been on the fringes of Amy's life, it had seemed to Sophia, spending most of his time at the office and then ensconcing himself in his study when he was home.

"He's like a ghost," Amy had joked once. *"You might hear the creak of a door or the rattle of a chain, but you never actually see anything."*

"Five years ago, Carl Leary and I had an affair."

"An—" Sophia tried to keep her jaw from dropping, but doubted she'd hidden her shock. "I—I had no idea."

Hope gave a shaky laugh. "Of course, we tried to keep our relationship a secret and thought we'd succeeded. We should have known better."

Sophia could almost hear the tumblers falling

into place, Hope's revelation the missing key to the past. "Amy found out."

The older woman nodded. "I don't know how, and it hardly matters. She knew. She was furious, and she had every right to be. Just like you have every right to be furious with me now."

The whirlwind of emotions spinning through Sophia made it almost impossible to settle on only one. "I—I don't know what to say."

"Carl and I knew back then you were telling the truth about the break-in. That Amy was the one responsible. We should have gone to the police right away. Instead, Carl and Marlene covered for Amy, and you took all the blame. I am *so* sorry, Sophia."

"So the offer to run the shop, that's what? Some kind of compensation?" Hurt, anger and disappointment took turns, striking out like a three-headed monster. "I lost my best friend, my father quit his job! I felt like the whole town turned against me and my only choice was to leave my family and the only home I'd ever known. But, hey, I get the keys to The Hope Chest as a consolation prize."

Stricken by the accusation, Hope whispered, "No, that's not it—that's not why I offered. I meant what I said. I thought you were the perfect person to take over when you first started working here. *Before* the break-in. And maybe trying to make up for what happened is a part of it, but I wouldn't ask if I didn't think you'd love running the store."

Everything happens for a reason.

Her father had been talking about his own life, but didn't his words apply here, too? Hadn't the years she'd spent away from Clearville, away from home and family, made her appreciate what she had even more?

If she'd never left town, if Hope had offered her the store five years ago, would she have realized what an amazing opportunity it was? Or would she have always wondered if there wasn't something more somewhere else?

Lifting the lid of the jewelry box, the tinkling melody began to play. A song that brought to mind Kansas, witches, shiny red shoes, and a land over the rainbow...

There's no place like home.

"I think you're right," Sophia said as the notes faded away. "I think I would love it."

Already she could picture the cradle set up in the corner, not on display, but in use as she brought her baby with her to work each day.

Hope's smile was tremulous but filled with her usual spirit. "I know you will, but if it helps you decide, we could give the arrangement a trial period. Say, for six months? Until your baby is born?"

After swearing Hope to secrecy on two counts—about her offer for Sophia to run the store and about Sophia's pregnancy—Sophia drove the other woman home. Although she'd already locked up for the day, she couldn't resist driving back to town where the shop—*her* shop?—waited.

"And don't forget," Hope had reminded her, "the apartment upstairs will be ideal once the baby comes. I think that hand-carved cradle would be perfect up there."

Sophia hadn't seen the upstairs apartment in years, but from what she remembered, the two-room unit with its tiny kitchenette and living space might be perfect for the two of them. Staying in Clearville would mean finding a place to live. As much as she loved her parents, she didn't want to move back into their house. She needed to make a home for herself and her baby.

She ignored the hollow spot in her heart, the empty place only Jake could fill. Would he be part of that life? She longed to talk to him about Hope's offer and the woman's revelations about Amy's motives for the break in, but she hadn't seen him all day. She missed him; one day apart and she missed him terribly.

Lost in her thoughts as she headed toward the shop, Sophia gave a startled apology as she bumped into someone coming out of the jewelry store next door. "Oh, I'm sorry…" Her words drifted away under Marlene Leary's icy glare.

"Do watch where you're going next time," the older woman advised.

Only a few days ago, Sophia would have ducked away from Marlene Leary's scorn, and even though her head was still reeling from Hope's revelations, Sophia felt…free. She'd always wondered why Amy had done what she had, but she hadn't realized how much not knowing had weighed on her. But now, everything made sense.

Knowing didn't change what Amy had done; it certainly didn't make it right. But Sophia could sympathize with what her friend must have been going through. Vandalizing The Hope Chest hadn't been another prank or a stupid dare. It had been a cry for help—one Amy's parents had smothered for the sake of their own reputations.

Marlene had already walked away when Sophia called out, "You're going to have to get used to running into me around here, Mrs. Leary."

Amy's mother slowly turned. "What is that supposed to mean?"

"Hope has asked me to take over the shop. It's a trial period for now, but if things work out—"

"No!" Marlene's heels clacked on the boardwalk as she marched back to face Sophia. "You can't move back here."

"This is my home. This is where my family lives." Clearville might be a small town and some of its residents held on to the past too long, but Jake was right. Sophia couldn't imagine raising her child anywhere else.

He'd convinced her to stay. Now the only question was, could she convince him to do the same?

"And what about Amy?" Marlene demanded. "This is her home, too! She hasn't come back—not once! And if you're here, she'll never—"

Her words cut off, but another piece of the puzzle fell into place. "Is that what you think? That if I move back, Amy won't come home? I've been gone for years, Mrs. Leary. I'm not the reason Amy's stayed away. But if you're worried, you can tell her I forgive her."

"*You* forgive her! You're the one who caused the whole mess in the first place."

Marlene had made the same accusation before, but the force behind the words, behind the woman herself, was missing, and Sophia could only feel sorry for her. The lies the Learys had told might have protected the family's good name and saved their marriage from scandal, but the deception had cost them their daughter.

"I forgive her," Sophia repeated, "and I understand."

Color leached from Marlene's face. "What is that supposed to mean?"

"It's time to let go of the past and move on." Too much time had happened to think she and Amy could ever be close again, but Sophia didn't want to be any part of the reason for her not to come home. "Tell Amy I've missed her. She was my best friend."

As Jake pulled up to The Hope Chest, he parked in the spot next to Sophia's little red car. Finding her vehicle wasn't enough to calm the worry building inside him. Sophia should have been home hours ago. The lights in the shop were out and the *Closed* sign on display in the front window.

Her parents had reassured him nothing bad ever happened in small-town Clearville, but Jake wasn't a small-town boy, and when it came to Sophia, he wasn't taking any chances. When his calls to the shop had continued to go straight through to the recording of Hope's voice asking him to call again another day, he'd grabbed his keys for the drive into town.

He'd told himself on the way over that the Pirellis were right. He was overreacting and Sophia had likely gotten caught up rearranging Hope's newest finds into another eye-catching window display, but as he walked toward the shop, he could see his own reflection in the darkened glass. Sophia wouldn't be working without the lights on. Still, he tried knocking on the front door, his unanswered pounding quickening his heartbeat. Where was she?

"Sophia!" His voice seemed to echo through-out the cool summer night.

Nothing. No lights flickering on, no movement or sound from inside.

Most of the other shops along the small board-walk looked equally deserted, but maybe Sophia had walked down to visit Debbie or one of the other shopkeepers. He'd taken a few steps toward the bakery when he glanced back at The Hope Chest and noticed something he'd missed.

A small rectangle of light shone in an overhead window.

Jake recalled Sophia telling him about an up-stairs apartment, and he breathed a sigh of relief. She'd gone upstairs, probably to hunt for some treasure Hope had stored up there, and lost track of time.

He'd noticed an outside staircase when he'd helped unload Hope's furniture delivery, so he circled around to the back of the store. She prob-ably had a perfectly good explanation for where she'd been, but Jake knew he wouldn't relax until he saw for himself that Sophia was okay.

He worried about her. About Sophia and about the baby. But seeing her in Clearville, surrounded by her family, was supposed to erase that worry, wasn't it? Hadn't that been the plan all along? Jake would convince Sophia this was where she belonged, and then he'd be free to go back to his own life, his conscience clear, his concerns assuaged.

But with each step that brought him closer to Sophia, Jake feared walking away wouldn't be so easy. Her family might be in Clearville, but what would happen when *he* was back home? When he wasn't there each morning to see her at breakfast? To stop by the shop in the middle of the day? To come home at night and listen to the events of her day?

What then? he wondered even as he realized the question wasn't so much what would Sophia do without him as how could he live without her?

Chapter Thirteen

The curtain inside the window fluttered, and the door opened before Jake had the chance to knock or turn and run from the realization hitting him like a punch to the gut. Or more accurately, a blow to the heart.

He was in love with Sophia.

Her short, dark hair gleamed beneath the faint porch light, and she wore a ruby-red blouse over a flared black skirt. The bright color made her skin glow, or maybe it was something radiating from inside, because he hadn't seen her so happy since they first met. She met his gaze with a huge smile, her dark eyes full of joy and free of the shadows that had haunted him since he told her the real reason why he'd been in St. Louis. The sight of it threatened to break through all his defenses, to snap the restraints of his control. He fisted his hands at his side to keep from pulling Sophia into his arms and pushing his way into the apartment beyond.

In the end, none of his valiant efforts at control made a difference. Because it was Sophia who grabbed his arms, Sophia who pulled him into the apartment, shutting the door behind them and locking out the rest of the world.

"You'll never guess what happened," she was saying, but Jake could barely concentrate on anything other than the knowledge that for the first time in a long time, they were completely alone.

"Hope wants me to run the shop. Not just while she's recovering, but from now on." She held out a hand as if to keep him from getting carried away. "It's only a six-month trial for now but…"

As her announcement sank in, Jake figured

Hope had stipulated the time limit to make Sophia more comfortable and not because the older woman had any doubts. Sophia loved working at the shop; he'd seen it in the way she carefully arranged a faceted crystal vase amid a dozen other vases, how she'd stepped back for a better view before moving close again to situate the piece a fraction of an inch, unwilling to settle until she found the perfect place.

He didn't need to take that step back to know Sophia had found her perfect place.

"Hope says she's lost her love for the shop, but I think—well, I think it's probably a number of things. Anyway, she says she wants to do more traveling, to look for antiques all over the country instead of only at local estate sales. It'll be great for her and great for the shop."

Excitement glowed in her cheeks, growing even brighter as she kept talking. "And look at this apartment. She says I can move in as soon as I'd like." Sophia waved a hand around the small place, a clear reflection of Hope's tastes with its shabby-chic living room, a combination of white wicker furniture and floral pillows, and the country casual kitchenette beyond. "Hope had been using the space for extra storage, but as soon as she heard I was coming home, she hired someone to clean everything out. I don't know how she does it," she said, touching the ring she wore on her middle finger, "but Hope just seems to know when things are the right fit."

And Sophia was the right fit for the shop. Jake was as certain of that as Hope. And this was exactly what he'd wanted for Sophia. For her to see that raising her baby in her hometown, surrounded by family and people who loved her was the best thing for the both of them.

His job was done; it was time for him to move on because that was what he did. He reunited families, completing the circle but was careful to always stay on the outside. He couldn't risk getting caught up in wanting to fit in where he didn't belong. He hadn't risked it, not since he'd failed so badly with Josh and Mollie.

"Jake?" Sophia called his name, her dark eyes

soft with emotion as if she could see through him as clearly as she'd seen through the glass window. As his gaze locked with hers, he remembered her brother's words from the night before. *Guys always do stupid stuff to impress the girl. It's a rule.*

It was a rule Jake had been doing his damnedest to break. He knew what Sophia had been trying to do the night before, what that walk down a very bumpy and bruised memory lane had been all about.

From the moment he met the elder Pirellis, Jake had instantly admired and respected the couple. No one could spend more than a few minutes with them before realizing the love and caring they had for each other and their children. Jake might not have had the best childhood, but that didn't mean he couldn't recognize good parents when he saw them. And he saw everything good in Vince and Vanessa Pirelli.

But Sophia had also showed him what was *real.* Her parents weren't superhuman; they couldn't keep their children wrapped in a protective force field so no harm ever came to them. They weren't able to turn back time to keep accidents from happening or capable of waving a magic wand and instantly healing all wounds any more than he could have with Josh.

But could he really believe that he wasn't a bad father? That if Josh's accident made him a bad parent, then he would have to hold the Pirellis and every other parent up by that same standard? A standard *no one* could pass?

"Sophia, I—"

His voice broke off as words failed him. There was so much he wanted to say, but he couldn't grasp hold of the storm of emotions swirling inside him.

And Sam was right; there were some rules a guy couldn't break. But impressing Sophia really wasn't on Jake's mind as he bent down in front of her. Showing her what he couldn't find the words to express, he pressed a kiss against her stomach and the baby nestled inside. A baby he wanted to be his in all the ways that counted.

"Oh, Jake."

Tears trembled on her lower lashes, but Jake pulled her into his arms before they had a chance to fall. As his mouth claimed hers, tasting all the sweetness, all the warmth, all the welcome that he'd missed, he swore he would never make her cry.

He'd spend the rest of his life making her happy, proving to her again and again that the trust she placed in him was as safe and secure as the child in her womb. The thought was firmly planted in his mind, but his body was edging too close to spinning out of control. Especially when Sophia rose up on tiptoe, her hands clutching his shoulders, her breasts soft yet sensitized against his chest, her hungry kisses tempting him beyond all reason.

She tasted like the mints sitting by the register at Hope's shop—a combination of cool and hot, sweet and spicy—and if he didn't stop now…

"Sophia, wait." He broke away from her kiss, from the soft sounds of need she made in the back of her throat. Her skin was flushed with passion, her lips swollen and tender from his kisses, her eyes so dark Jake thought he might get lost in their depths forever—

He swallowed hard. Sophia had already had one man take advantage of her during an emotional moment, and there was no way in hell he was going to do anything to make her think he was anything like that SOB Todd Dunworthy.

Still cupping her face, his thumbs brushing the corners of her lips, unable to completely break contact, Jake said, "Sophia, I can't."

A puzzled frown twitched her eyebrows, and he couldn't blame her for that confusion. Not when his body had already made it blatantly clear how much he wanted to. How desperately he wanted *her.* But then her expression cleared as she gazed up at him in that knowing way of hers, as if she could see right through him to all the empty places inside. As if she knew just how to fill them…

"Then let me."

His strangled laugh turned into a groan when her hands slipped beneath the hem of his shirt to find naked, needy skin. He still had it in mind to be noble, self-sacrificing, to see to Sophia's pleasure and not his own for this, their first time together. But she made that all too impossible because it wasn't *her* pleasure Sophia was after, but his…

Jake wasn't sure how they made it to the bedroom; all he knew was that when Sophia tumbled him backward, her eyes lit with laughter and arousal, he didn't hit the floor but instead sank into a snowy white quilt. Not that it would have mattered, he thought dimly as he rolled over, cradling Sophia beneath him. She was all the softness and comfort he would ever need.

Sophia had stripped off his T-shirt somewhere along the way, but some moments were meant to be savored. Like the slow slide of one button after another, revealing more and more of the heated flush on Sophia's skin. By the time he reached the final button on her shirt, Jake didn't have to part the material. The rapid rise and fall of her breathing did the job for him, allowing him to concentrate on removing the lacy bra beneath.

She was perfect. Gorgeous. More beautiful than he'd imagined. He murmured the words against the softness of her skin as he took her breast in his mouth. Sophia cried out, her hands fisted in his hair as she urged him on. Her skirt was little more than a ruffle of material easily off and away. His jeans were a little more of a challenge with Sophia's eager, arousing fingers making his own clumsy...and shaking.

Eventually he threw them aside, desire pounding through his veins, urging him on...but not yet. Not until he pressed his mouth against the slight swell of her belly without the barrier of material in the way. He felt her muscles clench and tremble against his lips. Before long, Jake hoped to feel the flutter and movement of the baby inside, and he knew...capturing Sophia's gaze as he rose up to sink into her softness, he knew that, no matter how impossible, the baby— like its mother—was his.

Sophia gazed up at Jake, her heart still pounding, her body still trembling, as he brushed the hair back from her eyes, his expression as tender now as it had been wild only moments ago.

I love you.

The words rose up, almost as impossible to stem as the tide of pleasure that had washed over her again and again as Jake had moved inside her, but she ruthlessly fought them back. It was the last thing Jake wanted to hear, and the first thing that would make him run.

He'd told her over and over that he wasn't a family man, and while she didn't believe it, Sophia needed time to change his mind. Time she wouldn't have if she scared him off after their first night together.

"Sophia," he began, his gaze—so serious, so intense—sending panic racing through her.

No, no…not yet! Terrified he was ready to start laying the groundwork for his way out of town so soon, she jumped in, desperate to hold on to some small piece of him that might one day grow into something more.

"Look, Jake, it's okay. Neither one of us expected this, not really, and it's a lot to take in. I know everything's happened so fast. You have your job in L.A. Your home and your family." When he would have protested, she touched her fingers against his lips. "They still *are* your family, Jake."

"So what are you saying?" he asked, his expression and the face she gazed at so intently during moments when she felt closer to him than she'd thought possible now an enigmatic mask. The molten fire in his golden eyes had hardened to cool metal, but Sophia forced herself to continue. She *couldn't* give up now. She had to at least try.

"My parents' party is in two days and after that—"

After that Jake was leaving.

It was the deal they'd made, but Sophia wanted to hold on as tightly as she had while they were making love and never let him go. She could already feel the cracks in her heart, hairline fractures threatening to break into gaping fissures as Jake pulled away.

Tears scalded the back of her throat, but she

forced a smile. "I'll be busy at the shop, and you have your work to get back to. But we can call and, maybe, in a few weeks, if you have time between cases, we can make plans to see each other."

"See each other," he echoed, his voice stiff and emotionless, and Sophia had the sudden feeling that she'd handled this all wrong.

She loved Jake so much, and she didn't care what kind of father figures he'd had; she knew the kind of father he would be. But she didn't want to push, didn't want to move too fast. After one night together, she couldn't possibly expect him to turn his whole life on end simply because she'd decided there was no place like home. She wanted to give Jake time. She would be willing to wait as long as he was willing to try, taking baby steps, until the three of them could be a family together.

"Yes, see each other," she repeated, but with less certainty this time. She was trying to make this as easy as possible, asking for as little as she could bear to take, but was even that too much?

Did Jake want to make a clean break and cut all ties when he left? Instead of a beginning, would tonight end up being the beginning of the end?

Heartsick, she waited for him to reject everything she was offering. Instead, after an interminable silence, he took a deep breath and nodded. "Okay, that's—okay."

Relief poured through her, leaving Sophia weak and trembling, her nerves as shaken as if she'd completed an emotional marathon. But the rush of triumph was missing even as Jake leaned forward, capturing her with his golden gaze a second before he claimed her lips in a possessive kiss. She reached out, but he was already pulling away.

Clearing his throat, he said, "We should get back to your parents' house. I think I got them a little worried when I couldn't get ahold of you."

"Oh, sure," Sophia blinked. The rush to get back home wasn't what she'd expected. Not when they could have spent more time alone together at the apartment. But as Jake stepped into the bathroom to give her a moment's privacy to dress, she repeated her new mantra as she gathered her shirt and skirt. Slowly pulling on each piece, she couldn't help but think of the rush and fervor of Jake stripping the clothes off her body.

But that moment was gone, and so too she feared was that passionate, soul-stealing side of Jake.

"Baby steps," she whispered with a glance at the closed bathroom door as she finished dressing. But when Jake silently walked her to her car a few minutes later, Sophia couldn't help feeling they'd somehow taken those steps in the wrong direction.

Standing on the Pirellis' porch, Jake sucked in a deep breath of cool summer air and waited for the peace of the quiet night to wash over him… and waited…and waited, *dammit!*

Slapping his palms down on the front railing, he gripped the wood until he feared leaving grooves in the grain. How had everything gone so wrong? How could he have held Sophia in his arms one moment only to listen in stunned silence as she was sending him on his way in the next?

She'd *call?* They would *see each other?* When they had time, of course, because she was *busy...*

It was Mollie all over again, Jake thought, his gut twisting at the truth he longed to deny. He wasn't outside of the family circle, but he certainly wasn't at the center, at the *heart* of Sophia's life where he wanted to be.

He couldn't live like that again—hovering on the periphery, teetering on the edge, one misstep away from being pushed out entirely. Not again.

Sophia didn't like the way she and Jake had left off the night before. For too brief a time, everything had been perfect. She'd come apart in his arms, the pleasure and passion of the moment surpassed only by the tenderness and emotion she'd seen in his eyes. He'd made her feel sexy and yet safe. Swept away by reckless desire, but anchored to solid ground.

And he made love like a man *in* love.

But then she'd had to ruin the fragile present with talk about the future.

She feared at this point anything she said might end up making matters worse, but she had to try. They only had one day left before her parents' party, and she wanted to spend it together without the shadow of expectations she'd cast hovering over them.

After dressing quickly in a pale-yellow blouse and a stretch denim skirt that she feared might not make it past another meal, Sophia headed down the hall. A glance in the guest bedroom revealed Jake's bed neatly made and not an item out of place. His woodsy aftershave lingered in the room, the scent alone enough to make the nerves in her belly quiver.

She found her parents sitting at the kitchen table, staring into their cups of coffee, but Jake wasn't there with them. The look her parents exchanged as she walked into the room had never boded well when she was growing up, and Sophia suspected it didn't now, either. "What? What's wrong?"

"We found a note this morning, sweetie. Jake left last night," her mother confessed. "He said there was something he had to do."

"He left?" The two words were more than Sophia could wrap her thoughts around as they spun through her head on a repetitive loop. *He left, he left, he left me...*

"Don't worry though. He'd said he'd be back tomorrow." Her dad was quick to reassure her, but Sophia could see by her mother's worried frown that Vanessa wasn't as certain.

Tomorrow. As far as her parents were concerned, tomorrow was simply another day. They didn't realize tomorrow was the anniversary party she and her brothers had been planning. The party she'd recently stopped dreading because she now had enough good news to far outweigh the bad.

But without Jake...

"What kind of boyfriend would I be if I missed your parents' anniversary party?" he'd asked her that first night.

I guess I'll have my answer, Sophia thought,

trying and failing not to feel like he'd already abandoned her. By this time tomorrow night, she'd find out what kind of boyfriend Jake was and if even her offer to slow their relationship down and take things one step at a time had been too much, too soon.

"Did something happen, Sophia?" her mother asked as Sophia sank into a kitchen chair.

Something had happened, all right. She'd made love with Jake, and he'd left. *Just like when she told Todd she was pregnant...*

Sophia shoved the comparison aside. Jake wasn't Todd. He wasn't.

"There's something I need to tell you."

Her parents exchanged another look, and Sophia swallowed hard. She could already feel the weight pressing down on her—the worry, the disappointment, the *Oh, Sophias* she'd avoided so far.

"Hope wants me to permanently take over running the shop," she blurted out.

"Oh, honey! Does that— Does that mean

you're moving back home?" her mother asked, hope and happiness written on her features.

"It does. I am." Sophia laughed as her father scooped her up in a hug just like he hand when she was a child.

Looking into her parents' smiling faces, Sophia saw their love for her as deeply ingrained as her father's dark hair and her mother's green eyes. It was part of their DNA and something that would never change, no matter what she did. She'd always known that, but only since she'd learned she was pregnant did she realize how overwhelming a love for a child truly was.

It was only one more day until their surprise party, but Sophia couldn't keep quiet any longer. She'd opened up to Jake the night before, and maybe he hadn't responded the way her heart longed for him to, but taking that chance had been the right thing to do.

Just like telling her parents the truth was the right thing to do.

"There's something else."

"More good news?"

"I hope you'll think so, Mom. I know I do." Taking a deep breath, Sophia said, "I'm going to have a baby." In the silence that followed, she added, "I'm pregnant."

"Oh, Sophia." Tears shimmered in Vanessa's eyes. "That's not good news—it's the best news! Isn't it, Vince?"

"Another grandbaby," he said gruffly. "Nothing better than that."

Tears stinging her eyes, Sophia asked, "So you aren't disappointed?"

Jake had promised her it would be like this— that her parents would understand and welcome her baby with open arms. He'd told her everything would work out.

"All we've ever wanted is for you to be happy," her mother reassured her.

"I am happy." Happy about the baby, about moving home, and about taking over The Hope Chest. She only needed one thing more for her happiness to be complete.

"We should call your brothers and let them know," her father announced. His smile was wide, but Sophia didn't miss the hint of steel that had kept their family in line for decades. "There's a new baby to celebrate, and when Jake *does* get back, we've got a wedding to plan."

Chapter Fourteen

Sophia thought constant motion might be the key to staying one step ahead of the heartache dogging her heels. If she kept moving, maybe the pain of Jake's leaving simply wouldn't have the chance to catch up. And with the final preparations for her parents' party underway, she had any number of last-minute details to keep her busy.

It was a good plan, and one that might even have a chance to work if she wasn't bumping into her brother every time she tried to dart here and there to oversee the rented tables and chairs, the decorations, the set up for the band, the food...

"Honestly, Nick!" Sophia complained as she ran into her oldest brother for the fourteenth time that morning—this time in the kitchen as she checked on the caterers. "Can't you just—be somewhere else right now?"

Drew had left with her parents early that morning under the guise of showing them the work he was doing on a custom house. To keep her parents from noticing three dozen or so strange cars parked in front of their house and figuring *something* had to be going on, Sam and some of his friends were playing valet, chauffeuring the guests' cars to a neighboring street while the guests gathered in the backyard to prepare for the big moment.

She'd counted on them to do their part; she hadn't counted on Nick hovering at her side, his solemn, dark-eyed concern threatening to trip her up, to slow her down until she had no choice but to face the reality of Jake's absence. "Sorry," Nick said, his tone 100 percent unapologetic, "but I'm in charge of making sure you don't overdo it." Despite their recent estrangement,

Nick had been as strong and supportive as Drew and Sam. Telling her parents about the baby had been like pulling on a single thread. Instead of snapping the loose piece off, her tightly woven secrets had started to unravel. In the end, she told her family all about Todd, about losing her job with the Dunworthys and about Jake.

Well, almost everything about Jake.

When the time comes, blame me. Tell them I'm not a family man.

His words played in her mind, but she couldn't stop and think about that right now or she'd never make it through the party without having some kind of breakdown.

Nick's lips curved in a shadow of his former smile. "You've got that look Mom gets when her head's about to explode."

"I'm fine. *Everything's* fine."

"Good. Then you can take a break and wait for Mom and Dad to get here." Sophia tried to protest, but Nick was already leading her out of the kitchen and into the backyard.

White tablecloths gleamed beneath a canopy

of twinkling lights. Fresh-cut flowers and the scent of candles filled the air. A stage, complete with dance floor, had been set up inside a tent, and the band waited in silence for their cue.

"Is Sam still out front taking care of the cars?"

"I talked to him a few minutes ago. Says he has it all under control," her eldest brother said wryly. "Which is never a good sign."

"I'm sure he'll do fine."

"And what about you?"

"What about me?"

Taking a deep breath, Sophia looked for something more to do, to change, to reorganize. But there was nothing. Her parents were on their way, and everything was perfect.

Almost perfect...

"Sam and Drew said it was your idea to book the Mediterranean cruise for Mom and Dad."

"I thought it was a good idea. Dad told me he'd always wanted to tour Italy."

Nick frowned. "He never said anything like that to me."

Glancing up at her brother, she said softly,

"Maybe he told me because he knew I'd understand. Because he knew I'd felt that same wanderlust, too."

She held her brother's gaze, waiting for him to see that the choices she'd made—right or wrong—had been her choices, but she would no longer take the blame for Carol's decisions.

"I'm sorry, Nick. I'm sorry Carol left, but my taking off for Chicago wasn't the reason she abandoned you, and I'm through feeling like it is. I—"

"I know."

Certain she hadn't heard him right, Sophia said, "What?"

"I know it isn't your fault. Carol made her own choice, and it wasn't me, and it wasn't Maddie. Sometimes—" his jaw clenched "—I get so angry that she could walk out like she did. But she's Maddie's mother and Maddie still loves her."

As her brother gripped the back of a chair, his shoulders bowed, Sophia wondered if maybe Maddie wasn't the only one. Hesitant to break the unexpected truce, Sophia cautiously asked, "Why didn't you go after her, Nick? As angry as you were when she left, maybe if you'd just talked to Carol..."

"I did. A few months after she left, I was in San Francisco for a seminar, only I went to see Carol instead. I told her I thought we should try to work things out, to give our marriage, our family a second chance, and if she disliked living in Clearville that much, I'd move to San Francisco."

Of all the things Nick could tell her, that was the last Sophia expected. She knew Nick loved his wife, but she wouldn't have thought he would consider leaving Clearville for anyone. "You did?"

"Yep. Told her I'd start a new practice there. I could work on pampered pets with larger wardrobes than my own." Nick grimaced at the thought of cats and dogs with diamond-studded collars.

"What happened?" she asked hesitantly, already knowing what *hadn't* happened. Nick hadn't moved to San Francisco and Carol hadn't come home.

At first, she didn't think he was going to answer, but finally he admitted, "Turns out Clearville wasn't the only thing Carol thought was small town."

"Oh, Nick. I'm so sorry."

"Not your fault, remember?"

"That doesn't mean I can't still feel bad for what you went through."

"I keep telling myself it's for the best."

"Maybe someday you'll actually start to believe it."

"Yeah, maybe." His gaze narrowed as if he was truly seeing her for the first time. "You've grown up, you know. You're not the little girl you used to be."

"'Bout time, huh?"

Her brother stayed quiet, his assent written in silence, but that was okay, because she could see the approval written there, too. "You're not so grown up that you don't need your big brothers, though."

"Oh, yeah?"

"Yeah. To do all the things big brothers do."

"What? Like to put frogs in my bed and pull my hair and make me eat spinach when Mom and Dad aren't here?"

"All that, and to kick your boyfriend's ass, too, for not being here."

"I've already told you, Jake isn't my boy-friend."

He'd told her to make him out to be the bad guy, but Sophia had made him the hero instead—a friend who'd come home with her to make telling her family about the baby she carried a little easier to bear.

"He's a friend," Sophia repeated now. "And he said he'd be here."

She'd been repeating the words for the past twenty-four hours. Twenty-four hours without word from Jake. He was running out of time, and she was running out of hope.

Nick started to reply when Sam raced around the side of the house, looking much as he had as a little kid on a Sunday morning—hair combed, shoes polished, dress clothes on, but still the same old Sam. "Everybody, get ready! Drew's pulling up right now!"

Her brother hadn't mentioned how he was going to get her parents around to the back of the house, but she could hear his voice getting loud as they drew closer. "I really think I should take a look at the back, Dad."

"Son, you're turning into a man who can't see beyond his job. There is nothing wrong with the roof." Vince came into view first, his gaze skyward, until the band started to play and the guests shouted, "Surprise!"

Her mother recovered first, lifting her hands to her face before embracing first her son and then her husband in a hug. Sam was next, swinging Vanessa around, almost as exuberantly as he did when he played with Maddie. By then, Nick and Sophia had reached the group.

"You did this! I can't believe you all did this!" Vanessa gushed, her eyes filling with tears.

"It was their idea," Sophia said of her brothers even as they credited her with most of the work. "But enough about that! Everyone is here to celebrate with the two of you."

Sophia and her brothers stepped back, letting longtime friends surround the elder Pirellis. Before long, someone had called out for a toast, and her red-faced, somewhat flustered parents made their way to the stage.

Vince stepped up to the microphone with Vanessa at his side. "First, I want to thank you all for coming here tonight and joining us in celebrating our marriage and our life together. It means so much that you all are here.

"I also want to thank my sons, who came up with the idea to try and give me and Vanessa heart attacks. This is amazing. Thank you."

Looking over the crowd, her dad gazed in Sophia's direction before glancing back at her mother and taking her hand with a huge grin. Sophia didn't think she'd ever seen her parents look happier and she…was *not* going to cry. She refused to cry.

"And last but not least, Sophia. Our little girl is home at last. You've already given us the best present by being here and by introducing us to your Jake."

The smile she'd practiced wearing all day suddenly felt frozen, stiff, ready to shatter into a dozen broken pieces. She could feel all eyes turning her way as Vince said Jake's name. But how could she blame her father? Drew had kept her parents away from the house all day. That was the plan. They had no way of knowing Jake hadn't kept up his end of the deal.

It was the past repeating all over again. Someone she cared about—worse, someone she *loved*—leaving her to pick up the pieces, to try to explain.

And dammit if she wasn't about to cry!

"It has been nearly forty years since your mother and I fell in love," her father continued, "but I still remember how that feels. I remember every time I look in my wife's eyes, and I remember when I look at Sophia and Jake together." He lifted his glass. "So I'd like to propose a toast. To my lovely wife, Vanessa, for the happiness she has brought to me during our marriage, and to Sophia and Jake for all their happiness still to come."

The toast echoed all around her until the words found a rhythm with her breaking heart. *Sophia and Jake...Sophia and Jake...*

The tables seemed to start to spin around her like the teacup ride at Disneyland, and she took a step toward the stage with a somewhat crazed idea of taking the microphone and announcing to one and all that there was no Sophia and Jake; there never had been a Sophia and Jake; there never would be a Sophia and Jake—

A masculine hand holding a champagne flute reached in front of her before she could take a second step. "You'll need a glass if you're going to drink to our toast."

Sophia spun around so quickly, she knocked into Jake's arm, spilling some of the apple juice onto the sleeve of his pale-blue dress shirt. He set the glass aside and shook some of the liquid from his hand. "Wasn't quite the way I planned it."

Reality sinking in that Jake was back, that

he'd come back, Sophia snapped out of the momentary shock into a flurry of motion. "Sorry, I'm sorry." She took the second flute from his hand, set it aside and grabbed a napkin from a nearby table to start dabbing at the spot left by the juice.

"You're supposed to drink it, Jake, not wear it!" Sam called out and Sophia realized her parents, her family, *everyone* had known Jake was standing behind her throughout the entire toast.

Standing behind her the entire time.

The urge to escape, to run in any direction, pulled at Sophia until she thought she might break apart. But then Jake reached out and took her hand, and everything inside her settled and stilled, disjointed pieces coming back together again.

Giving up on drying off his sleeve, Sophia snatched back her hand, took the napkin and hit him across the chest with the flimsy fabric. "Give me one good reason why I shouldn't have my brothers beat the *crap* out of you right now!"

After a brief tug of war with the napkin, Jake set it aside and led Sophia away from the rest of the party toward the gazebo she'd decorated with garlands of silk flowers for pictures later in the evening.

Sitting down, Jake pulled Sophia beside him. "I went to see Mollie."

His ex-fiancée?

"Not a very good reason," she whispered.

"I needed to see Josh." He clenched her hands as he silently pleaded with her to understand. "I know what you said about accidents happening, but I needed to see for myself that he was okay. That maybe I hadn't screwed up so bad that I don't deserve a second chance."

"Did you get to see him?"

His heartbreaking smile told her the answer. "Yeah, I saw him. He—he remembers me."

"Of course he does. You were part of his life for three years."

"I know, but he was so little, and I wasn't sure. But he remembers. He even remembered the accident and had to show me how much better he is at riding a bike now—without training wheels."

"I'm sorry, Jake. I know that was something you wanted to teach him."

"You know, it's okay," he insisted, even though she could see how the loss had wounded him a little. "I'm glad Mollie even let him look at another bike, let alone ride one. But...she's different now. Happier and more relaxed. She really does love Roger. She admitted that she'd wanted to get back together with him when we were together. The accident was the impetus she needed to tell him how she felt."

Sophia wasn't ready to forgive the other woman so quickly until Jake added, "She said it would be okay for me to still see Josh once in a while. Kind of like an honorary uncle." Happiness and hope shone in his eyes as he added, "If you don't mind."

Mind? That he could love another man's child so much?

"No," Sophia whispered, "I don't think I'd mind that at all."

"Well, then, I hope you don't mind if I tell you your plan for us to see each other pretty much sucks."

Sophia gaped at him in shock. "What?"

"I don't want to *see* you. I don't want to play phone tag or try to fit our relationship in when I have time." Anger sparked in his golden eyes, and Sophia realized that was what he'd been hiding the night in the apartment above the shop. Frustration, not that she'd asked for too much, but that she had expected so little.

She'd forced him to the sidelines of her life, the same way Mollie had even though it was never what she'd intended. "Oh, Jake. I am so sorry. I thought if I didn't ask for too much, then maybe I'd have a better chance of holding on to at least a part of you. But you're right. That never would have worked because the truth is, I want it all. Lover, husband, father, friend… everything."

"It's yours. I'm yours. I love you, Sophia. I spent years thinking I wasn't a family man, but the truth is, I'm like one of those dusty old things on Hope's shelves, just waiting for the right woman to come along."

"You're not so dusty or so old."

"But you are the right woman for me. You and your baby are the family I've been waiting for my whole life. Marry me, Sophia. Let's make this real."

Sweet, swift happiness rushed through her. "Yes, I'll marry you."

His kiss was filled with promise as he pulled her into his arms. "I love you," she whispered as he lifted his head. From the yard behind them, she could hear the sounds of the celebration continuing—for one lifetime of love thirty-five years in the making and for another lifetime just beginning.

As if picking up on her thoughts, Jake said, "We better do this pretty quick. Your parents already have thirty-five years on us. If we don't start soon, we'll never catch up."

"Oh, we'll get there," Sophia vowed with a smile. "Just wait."

* * * * *